SOUTHERN POISON

SHAUNA JARED

SHAUNA JARED

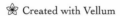

Jeff and Gunnar. I love you both more than you'll ever know. Thank you for always supporting me.

To my alpha and beta readers – Alana, Trish, Shawna, Kate, Erica, Klaudia – thank you for reading and for your feedback and support. I couldn't do it without you!

CONTENTS

CHAPTER 1

Ace

"*I*'ll see your ten K and raise ten more."

I tossed my chips onto the poker table, a cigarette dangling from my lips, which curled into a smirk. I glanced at the other men seated around me, all studying their cards while smoke swirled around, dancing in the dimly lit backroom. Andre tilted his head, narrowing his eyes at me from across the table, then studied his own hand as he took a drag from the cigar he held between his fingers. A hot blonde chick approached me, leaning in close while pressing her shapely body into mine, stirring a visceral reaction in me. I cut my eyes to her. Low cut, tight red dress. Tits to die for. Legs for days. *Later*, I told myself, trying to concentrate on the cards.

Andre rubbed the stubble on his jaw and raised a dark eyebrow at me. "You sure you wanna do that, Ace?" he asked in a deep Southern accent. A round of chuckles came from the others seated around the table as they waited for my reply, looking at me incredulously. Smoke bloomed above our heads, and only the dull thud of the bass from the main dance floor infiltrated the silence. The backroom of the nightclub, Indigo, was full of Nashville's most important players—at least according to Andre, who owned the club and handpicked the players himself. Their snickering died down as they glanced from me to Andre, each of them with either a cigar, a drink, or a woman—some all three. I took a pull from my cigarette, then slowly exhaled a cloud of smoke in Andre's direction.

"I'm sure." I felt the blonde's hand on my leg, slowly making its way up my inner thigh. She pushed her barely covered breasts into my bicep, making her intentions clear. I shot her a wink while the others folded one after another, leaving only Andre and me in the game.

He tossed back his tumbler of whiskey, giving me an amused glance as he set the empty glass down. The redhead hanging on his arm whispered something in his ear, her red lips curling into a devilish grin, which made him chuckle. He tilted his head at me.

"I hate to do it to you, man," he drawled. Sneering, he threw his cards down on the table. Some of the others gasped while I shook my head with a rueful smirk. A royal flush. The son of a bitch had a royal flush.

"Damn, Andre. If I didn't know any better, I'd think you stacked the deck." I tossed my cards down—four of a kind. Not good enough; I should've known better than to stay in.

He narrowed his eyes at my comment, and his goon in the corner made a move towards me. Andre held up a hand to stop him. His steely gaze locked with mine.

"He's talking out of his ass. The one he just lost to me." Another round of laughs. I took a pull from my whiskey, letting the sweet, spicy liquid burn its way down my throat. My family's own, "White Wolf." I snickered at the irony; I just blew twenty grand of my father's money while getting drunk on his whiskey. Wouldn't dear old Dad be proud?

I chuckled, putting my cigarette out in a nearby ashtray. "You've got my card on file. Put it on my fucking tab." Andre and his friends roared with laughter. Blondie rubbed herself against me again, and I felt my cock twitching mercilessly. I looked at her—long blonde hair hanging loose, her blue eyes burning with desire. She bit her pouty lower lip and dropped her gaze before looking up at me through thick, fake lashes.

I let my gaze travel over her perky tits, tiny waist, and curvy hips before settling on her eyes again. *Yeah, she'll do for the night.*

Andre smiled slyly as the dealer began setting up another game. "You in for another round, Dalton? See if you can win daddy's money back?" he asked. I threw back what was left of my drink, ignoring him. I turned to the blonde, still glued to my side, her hand only inches away from my cock. Later had turned into now.

"Let's go."

Callie

WHY THE HELL DID I AGREE TO THIS?

I sat at the bar, nursing a bottle of beer, while the other girls were dancing together or grinding against some random guy they just met on the dance floor, each of them wearing custom-made t-shirts declaring their role as bridesmaids, along with plastic, light-up tiaras. I glanced around the dimly

3

lit bar, hoping I wouldn't meet anyone's eye who might interpret that as a green light to approach me. Indigo was a popular club, and it was packed tonight. Bodies upon bodies were everywhere, moving to the music which thrummed relentlessly while strobe lights flashed, keeping up with the tempo.

Sarah, my best friend since childhood, had wanted to have her bachelorette party here. So. Here we were. And I was counting the minutes until it was over.

I sighed and took a pull from my lukewarm beer. This wasn't my scene. Not since I broke up with Vic, anyway. I would've paid good money to be back at my house working on my latest painting right now instead of sitting here in this club, pretending to have a good time. Who was I kidding? I wasn't even trying to pretend. I figured I'd give it another hour, then make some excuses to Sarah before heading home.

"Oh my God, Callie, why aren't you dancing with us?"

Speak of the devil. Sarah plopped down breathlessly on the bar stool beside me, her tiara askew, as was the sash she wore which proclaimed her as the "BRIDE." She shot me a drunken half-smile while she tried to rearrange her accessories.

I raised an eyebrow at her. "Have you met me? Hi, I'm Callie. I don't dance."

She frowned. "Oh no, you're not having fun!" She clutched her necklace full of tiny flashing penises, the corners of her little bow-shaped mouth turning down. The only appropriate word to describe Sarah was "cute," with her small stature, delicate features, bright blue eyes, and golden blonde hair. She resembled a little doll I used to have when I was a kid, in fact. She was the exact opposite of me, the one everyone dubbed "Amazon woman."

I groaned. "I'm having fun," I lied. I didn't want Sarah

to feel bad at her own bachelorette party. She was supposed to be having the best night of her life, her last night as a single woman before marrying the man of her dreams. She didn't need to be worried about whether I was enjoying myself.

Sarah rolled her eyes at me. "You're a terrible liar, babe."

I laughed, shaking my head. "Okay, fine, you're right. I'm miserable."

Sarah smiled slyly, cocking her head towards a guy sitting a few barstools away. "This guy has been checking you out for a while. If you'd let yourself, you could have a lot of fun tonight, babe." She winked at me while waving the bartender over.

I rolled my eyes at Sarah and sighed. I looked away from her, careful to avoid making eye contact with the guy she was referring to. I'd noticed him already; he was indeed checking me out. I wasn't interested, though, and nobody seemed to understand that, least of all Sarah. Sarah was in love and marrying one of the last good guys on the planet. How could she understand what I went through with Vic? Why I'd never want to go there again?

I sighed as the bartender brought back a fruity drink with an umbrella for my friend. I felt bad about being a Debbie Downer on her special night and figured I'd better make an effort. "Look, I'm gonna go freshen up, then I'll join you girls on the dance floor for a bit before heading home. Sound good?"

Sarah threw her arms around me, giving me a tight squeeze. "Yes! You're not going home either, but we'll start with getting you on the dance floor for now!"

I disentangled myself from her embrace with a laugh and grabbed my purse. I watched as Sarah found one of the other girls, then the two of them made their way back out onto the crowded dance floor.

I wandered through a throng of sweaty, gyrating bodies to the ladies' room. Two women came stumbling out, laughing their asses off. I raised an eyebrow at them and had gotten no more than three steps inside the bathroom when I knew exactly what they'd been howling about.

A loud moan came from one of the stalls, a woman's voice, slurred and euphoric. "Yes, yes, yes, Ace!" she cried as I quickly made for the sink. I cringed and laughed silently, unable to stop listening as she continued. Another woman exited a stall, doubled over with laughter. We shared a look as she left while the groaning and heavy breathing continued. I turned on the cold water and splashed a little on my face while the moans became louder, and a male voice joined in.

"Oh yeah, Michelle," he said, and I rolled my eyes at my reflection, stifling a giggle. *Wow, Ace and Michelle are really having a good time. Good God, people actually do this?* I grabbed some paper towels, shaking my head while drying my hands and face. I examined my hair briefly before exiting the bathroom, the moans and exaltations to God from the couple in the stall becoming quieter now.

Just as I was leaving, I heard the woman say, breathlessly, "My name's Becky, not Michelle." I snorted, unable to contain my laughter, and headed in the direction I last saw Sarah so I could get this over with and go home.

Ace

I TOSSED A COUPLE OF HUNDRED DOLLAR BILLS AT THE cab driver before stumbling out of the taxi onto the driveway of my parents' mansion. By now, the sun was rising, and I'd been gambling, drinking, and fucking Michelle slash Becky all night long. Whatever her name was, the platinum blonde sat inside the taxi with the window rolled down, pointing and laughing, when I stumbled and nearly fell.

"You're so fucked up, Ace. Oh my God!" she said, giggling. Her ruby red lipstick was smeared, thanks to me, and her black eyeliner was smudged across her cheeks. With a whoop, she tossed a black bolero hat out the window, which landed on the entryway in front of the huge iron gate. She leaned out the back passenger side window of the taxi, still laughing, her massive tits on full display.

I bent down, grabbed the hat, and stuck it on my head while watching the car pull away. "Until we meet again, my dear Michelle," I called in a terrible, drunken attempt at a British accent. She blew me a kiss as the taxi backed out of the driveway.

"It's Becky!" she called back to me. Little did she know, I had no intention of ever meeting her again, no matter what her name was.

I groaned. At twenty-eight years old, I knew I was getting too old to pull all-nighters, although I'd never admit it to anyone. My head pounded, and the rapidly rising sun blinded me. I squinted and raised a hand to shade my eyes when I heard footsteps approaching.

"You'd better get your shit together, and quick, Ace. Mother's expecting us in the study soon," my brother, Jasper, the golden child of the family said. The youngest son who could do no wrong in our parents' eyes. I scowled at all three of him I saw when I looked in his direction.

"Hi, Jas," I slurred. He and I could've almost passed for

7

twins in our younger years. He had sandy blond hair and blue eyes like mine, but these days he had a boyish look about him I no longer had. He didn't have nearly as many tattoos as I did, and he cared way more about what our parents thought of him than I did, too.

A shock of his blond hair fell over one eye as he peered at me. He frowned, taking in my current state. "She won't be happy about this."

I laughed bitterly. "When is she ever happy?"

"Come on," he said, steadying me when I threatened to take a tumble.

"Fuck her and her family meetings," I muttered, letting Jasper shuffle me up the drive to the house, one arm holding me steady. "It's bullshit. BULLSHIT!" I yelled as we approached the front of the looming mansion, drawing the attention of the landscaping crew, who were busy trimming Mother's rose bushes.

Jasper shushed me. "God, you smell like a fucking ashtray. Where the hell have you been all night?" He pulled a face, turning away in disgust as we entered the foyer.

The maid, who had been dusting the ornate mirrors in the entryway, took one look at us and rushed off. I watched her go, admiring how her uniform hugged her curves as she went. I made a mental note to find her later. I turned my attention back to my brother.

"I've been living my best life, Jasper," I slurred, staggering a bit. I put a hand out to brace myself against the wall until I regained my balance.

"Whatever. Something's up, but I'm not sure what's going on." Jasper paused, one hand steadying me while stepping back a bit to appraise me. "You look awful, but there's not much to be done about it now. Come on," he said, turning me around and motioning for me to follow him to the study.

I looked down at myself. I wore a pair of Monfrere skinny jeans, a black Armani button-down shirt, untucked with the sleeves rolled up to show my tattooed forearms. I took the bolero hat off and flung it onto a nearby table as I followed Jasper. I glanced into the mirror the maid had been dusting as we passed by; my brother had a point. I looked like hell. My sandy blonde curls were a mess, and the bags under my eyes were bigger than the bags Mother took on her annual trips to Italy.

"Michelle thought I looked 'sexy AF'. Her words, not mine, bro," I muttered, trying to walk in a semi-straight line behind Jasper.

We heard a chorus of muffled conversation coming from the study before we reached it. I rolled my eyes as I heard Dad's distinct baritone voice behind the door. The tone of it rose and fell harshly, and I wondered what he was talking about. It sounded like he was in the mood to rip someone a new one, and I didn't need three guesses to figure out who that person was going to be. Jasper opened the door and all but pushed me inside.

"Well, there you are," our mother said, sitting on the couch next to our father's desk, wearing a grey twin set and white pants. Her silver hair was styled in a neat bob, and, setting her teacup on the small end table next to her, she turned her disapproving gaze to me. She narrowed her eyes, a nervous smile playing on her lips as she glanced between my father and me.

"Glad you could join us," Nick said with a smirk. My older brother sat in the corner with a cigar and today's edition of *The Tennessean*. He wore a three-piece suit, although it was a Saturday morning, looking sharp as usual. Didn't surprise me, daddy's little protege always made sure to look the part.

Jasper took a seat next to our mother, who patted his

leg affectionately. Mommy's favorite, taking his place of honor. That just left me, the black sheep. The family embarrassment. Bitterly, I went for a wingback chair that faced our father and flopped down in it, propping my sneaker-clad feet up on the edge of his desk. "I'm here. Let's get the party started," I said.

The room went silent, everyone watching Dad and me. I cocked my head to one side and smirked at him, crossing my arms, waiting for the lecture to begin.

Dad's eyes bored into mine, and after a few awkward moments, I was tempted to turn away. But I didn't; I wouldn't give him the satisfaction. "Horace. I hate to disappoint you, but this is not a party." *Horace*. I hated it when he called me by my given name. Everyone else called me Ace, but not him.

I chuckled, looking around at the somber faces of my brothers and mother. "Yeah, looks more like a funeral. And I'm guessing it's mine?" I met his disapproving stare again. "What did I do this time to bring shame upon the mighty Dalton name, Dad?" I could probably answer that question myself, and my version of the story would have been much more entertaining.

Dad smiled at me, which was unsettling. I could probably count on one hand the number of times I'd seen the old bastard smile in my whole life. I watched as he rose from his desk, using his cane to make his way around to me.

"You think you're so goddamned funny, don't you, boy?" Dad said in his deep, southern accent, then used the cane to knock my feet off his desk. The great Augustus Dalton, CEO of Dalton Enterprises, that was my dear old pops. Even in his late 70s, he still had a formidable presence about him, despite his appearance. He hunched over a bit as he held onto the cane, his snowy hair perfectly coiffed, his jowls sagging. He wore a navy Armani blazer, matching pants, and a white button-up shirt. A huge, flashy watch adorned his wrist. I didn't think I'd ever seen the man dressed down; he was always in business mode.

Our dad had started a family later in life, being so focused on his career and producing the best whiskey money could buy, he couldn't be bothered with worrying about marriage and children. Eventually, he realized he needed someone to carry on his empire, so he found a suitable wife, twenty years younger, to give him a few heirs. Now, here we all were, one big, happy, dysfunctional family.

I cut my eyes to Jasper, who stared at Dad with wide eyes. I noticed Nick's cocky half-grin as he folded the paper he had been reading, laying it on the side table. Mother clutched her pearl necklace, open-mouthed. I knew she wouldn't say anything, though. She had never stood up for me before. Why start now?

"This family could use a sense of humor, don't you think?" I asked, propping one ankle up on the opposite knee and leaning back in the chair. Dad's face went red and a tiny blood vessel in his forehead throbbed as he watched me.

"Are you eighteen or twenty-eight?" he asked, his voice growing louder as he continued. "You pissed away two years of college at Vanderbilt before dropping out, and now you can't be bothered to wake up before noon most days. You don't give a shit about this family or the company. You're too busy partying and gambling all my money away. Making scenes for the press to report the next day and messes for my lawyers to clean up," he said bitterly, standing before me, glaring in my direction. I didn't bother to meet his gaze or reply. Instead, I became preoccupied with picking some lint off my jeans.

He coughed and pulled a handkerchief out of the pocket

of his blazer, which he hacked into for another minute. We all waited in silence, knowing he wasn't finished berating me. It had become a ritual at Mother's damned family meetings — Dad praising Nick and Jasper, then jumping my ass for one reason or another. I was having trouble keeping my eyes open at this point. I just wanted him to finish the lecture so I could go the fuck to bed already.

"Augustus, please—" Mother began, but Dad held one hand up to silence her.

"It's high time you grew up, Horace," he said without looking at me, shoving the handkerchief back into his pocket. "That's why I'm cutting you off. No more credit cards. No more gambling, no more partying, and no more girls. It's over. You're going to work at Dalton Enterprises. You'll earn a paycheck and learn how this company works."

That got my attention. I abandoned my lint picking and looked up at him. Surely he was joking, right? "What?" I asked. It was the only word I could summon at this point. I could see Nick trying to stifle a laugh out of the corner of my eye.

"You heard me. Starting now." Dad turned away from me to face Nick. "I don't know what you're laughing about. Or you." He whipped around and pointed the cane at Jasper, who blinked in rapid succession. This was about to get interesting.

"All three of you need to grow the hell up," he boomed. Nick's jaw dropped, and I felt a soft smile playing on my lips.

"Grow up? I haven't missed a day of work since I graduated college," Nick spat, throwing a glance in my direction in a silent jab at me.

Dad wore a false smile as he turned his steely gaze on Nick. "You're right. It's your attitude that's the problem."

With one hand, I shielded the grin that spontaneously

erupted across my face as I watched Nick turn red. I couldn't believe what I was hearing, but I was living for it.

"My 'attitude?'" Nick asked with an incredulous look.

"You treat everyone around you like they're a piece of goddamned gum you found stuck on the bottom of your shoe. You can't run a multi-million dollar company with that kind of attitude, Nicholas," Dad said, his voice calmer and steadier now. "The press has a field day every time you fire an assistant for getting your coffee wrong. It projects the wrong image, and I won't have it any longer. I believe the last headline was 'Nicholas Dalton—the devil in a Brioni suit.'"

Nick's mouth was set in a hard line, his jaw muscles clenching. I could tell he was fighting with everything in him not to let go with a scathing retort, which would only prove Dad's point.

Apparently finished with Nick, Dad turned to Jasper. Mother grabbed Jas's hand and squeezed. Her sweet little baby was about to get a tongue lashing too; Dad was leaving no stone unturned today, it seemed. I actually hated it for Jasper; of the three of us, he was least deserving of Dad's wrath.

"First of all, Evelyn, you need to cut the apron strings. You've coddled that boy for far too long, made him weak and timid. No place in business for the weak, boy," Dad said, his gaze landing on Jas, whose face flushed as he spoke.

"Augustus! How dare you say such things!" Mother exclaimed, promptly letting go of Jasper's hand. Dad wasn't entirely wrong. Jas had always been Mother's favorite, being the youngest. Shy and lacking self-confidence? Yes, a bit. But weak? Nah, Dad had that part wrong. There would be no telling him that, though.

"You know it's true, woman. Jasper, time to grow up

and prove you can help run this company with your broth-ers," Dad said, narrowing his eyes. Then he turned to sweep us all with his icy gaze, using his cane to swivel about.

"All of you. Grow the hell up. Otherwise, I'll sell this goddamned company and donate the proceeds to charity before letting the three of you run it into the ground after I'm gone. Now. Go on and leave me be," he said in a somber tone, making his way back behind his desk, where he sat down heavily in his enormous leather chair.

"But we haven't even—" Mother started, but Dad silenced her with a look. She glanced at the three of us and shrugged softly, wringing her hands in her lap.

"Fine by me." I didn't waste any time getting the hell out of there. As entertaining as it had been to hear Dad scolding Nick and Jasper for a change, I'd heard more than enough. Cut me off? That's how the bastard wanted to play? I jerked the study door open roughly, letting it hit the wall as I exited the room without another look at any of them.

Callie

I STUDIED THE PAINTING ON MY EASEL WITH A SCOWL while chewing on the end of my paintbrush. Something was wrong, but I couldn't put my finger on it. I dabbed at the Burnt Sienna on my palette and added a few brush strokes to the canvas, cocking my head as I chose precisely where to add the color. It was mid-morning, and I was upstairs in my bedroom with the huge half-circle window above the bed. Light streamed in, filling the room with a golden aura and casting shadows on the walls. This was my favorite room for painting because of the natural light from the large window, so I kept a small easel and duplicates of my favorite painting supplies in here for moments like these.

My long, dark brown hair was pulled up in a messy bun, and I wore only an extra long t-shirt and socks. Led Zeppelin blared from the speakers as I worked on the painting—a field of sunflowers with a setting sun in the background—pinks, purples, and blues swirling on the canvas to depict the sunset above the hues of yellow, gold, and brown sunflowers. My favorite flower. The reference photo was taped to the wall nearby, and to the average person, my painting probably looked like an exact duplicate of the photo. But to me, it wasn't right yet. It wasn't perfect.

My phone rang, startling me out of my trance. I turned off my music and picked the phone up, rolling my eyes when I saw who was calling.

"*Grand-Mère*, how are you?" I put the paintbrush and palette down, feeling the inspiration draining from my body as I waited for my grandmother to speak. Lately, her calls brought me nothing but guilt, accusations, and despair, and I was sure this one would be no different.

"Caroline. Am I to expect you for tea this afternoon then?" As always, Grand-Mère skipped the pleasantries and got right down to business. Her thin voice, seasoned with the remnants of a French accent, grated on my nerves today. I smiled in preparation to answer her, hoping to avoid yet another argument.

"Of course, *Grand-Mère*. We always have tea on Saturday afternoons, don't we?"

She huffed. "Good. I have something *très important* to discuss with you, ma chère."

I rolled my eyes and stifled a groan. I knew exactly what she wanted to discuss; the trust my parents left to me

15

and how I was failing miserably at meeting the criteria to claim it.

Caroline Harrison, eligible to receive full funding of the trust set aside for her by her parents, Benjamin and Adele Harrison, upon her thirtieth birthday, must have also entered into marriage by this date or shall forfeit any claim to said inheritance.

I sighed.

My parents had died in a car accident when I was twelve years old. I remembered coming home from school one day with Grand-Mère waiting for me, tears in her eyes. She explained as gently as she could so that twelve-year-old me could understand that my parents were gone and were never coming back. My entire world had changed in the blink of an eye. The most important people in my life had been ripped away, leaving a gaping hole in my heart that would never be filled again.

After a few years, it had gotten easier, although I still missed them like crazy. I lived with Grand-Mère, who made sure I had the best of everything—the best schools, clothes, toys, friends. Anything I wanted, she made sure I had it. I had always thought she was trying to make up for my parents being gone. She'd been my rock, my shelter from the storm, and my guiding light as I grew up. But now that I was grown, things had taken a turn in our relationship.

Grand-Mère was hell-bent on me finding a husband before I turned thirty so I could inherit the money my parents had left in the trust for me. My father's family had been wealthy but wanted nothing more to do with him after he married a common French newcomer instead of the local socialite they'd handpicked for him. After the marriage, they'd given him his birthright and washed their hands of him. With what he'd been through, his own family rejecting him because of his marriage choice, I wondered why on earth he would put such criteria as marriage on my inheritance? Shouldn't he have wanted me to have the money whether or not I was married? Shouldn't my happiness have been the most important thing to my parents? It had never made any sense to me.

But for the past few years, it was all Grand-Mère could think about. She was constantly sending me news articles about some local bachelor from a wealthy family or trying to set me up on blind dates. It was exhausting, and it was wearing our relationship thin.

Why should I have to be married to inherit what belonged to me? What if I didn't want to be married? The trust fund and the looming deadline of my thirtieth birthday had been hanging over my head like the blade of a guillotine for so many years that I had all but given up any hope of ever collecting my inheritance. Now, at twenty-eight years old, Grand-Mère had taken it upon herself to put the husband search into overdrive on my behalf.

"*Grand-Mère*," I began, shaking my head, although she couldn't see me. I wanted to tell her I'd be fine without the money. I'd make my own way in the world, on my own terms. I wasn't about to marry some virtual stranger just to collect the money. I had a college degree, and I'd been supporting myself just fine doing freelance art commissions. But I'd said those things before, and she never listened.

"There's a fundraising event coming up that we have to attend, ma chère. We'll discuss the details over tea. Please be on time." And with that, she hung up, leaving me staring at my phone in disbelief.

A fundraising event? She actually wanted to talk about something other than my non-existent impending nuptials? I breathed a sigh of relief, a small smile playing on my lips. To have tea with her and not spend an hour talking about the desirable qualities I should look for in a husband? It would be like old times, back when the deadline was only a speck on the horizon. What a welcome relief it would be to visit with her and not have her badgering me about settling down.

I grinned, placing my phone on my desk while retrieving my paintbrush. I looked at my sunflower painting and instantly knew where I should add some highlights to make it really pop. I grabbed a tube of paint, humming to myself, as I squeezed some Titanium White onto my palette and went back to work.

I ARRIVED AT GRAND-MÈRE'S HOUSE IN GREEN HILLS a few minutes early, knowing how much she appreciated promptness. This was the house I'd grown up in after my parents died, a charming little white brick ranch-style home. Nothing fancy, but its location meant it was worth a lot of money these days. I had told Grand-Mère many times she should sell it and buy a place closer to me, but she wouldn't hear of it. Probably because the house held so many memories of her long-dead husband, my Grand-Père, and of my mother as a girl.

I got out of my Mustang and smoothed the wrinkles out of my skirt while mentally preparing myself for tea with Grand-Mère. She had said she wanted to talk about a charity event, and as nice as that sounded, I figured that eventually, the conversation would circle back around to finding me a husband. It always did.

I sighed and walked up the driveway to the house, where Grand-Mère stood at the door, waiting for me with a stern look on her face. She was a tall, willowy woman with dark brown hair like mine, shot with streaks of gray, in her 70s, but she looked much younger, her skin relatively wrinkle-free. Her deep blue eyes fixed on mine, one eyebrow raised as I approached. As I did on many occasions, I felt as if I was peering into a time portal, getting a glimpse of a future version of myself. I had inherited much of my looks from my mother's side of the family, such as my height, build, mahogany-colored hair, and midnight blue eyes. I could only hope I remained as beautiful and youthful as Grand-Mère when I reached my 70s.

"Bonjour, Grand-Mère," I said, reverting to the French she'd made sure I learned while growing up. I wasn't fluent by any means, but I knew enough to get by when we traveled to France to visit relatives, which made her happy.

She hugged me, pulling me in for kisses on each cheek. "Caroline, come in, ma chère."

I squeezed past her into the sparsely decorated living room. In muted tones of cream, pink, and yellow, it had a subdued but cheerful aura. Sunlight streamed into the room through a large window, creating a box of light on the carpet where Grand-Mère's cat, Lucy, lay curled in a ball. A tray holding teacups and cookies already sat on the coffee table where steam rose from them, the aroma inviting me closer.

"Sit," she instructed, motioning towards the couch. I did as she asked, waiting while she passed a hot cup of tea to me.

"So, tell me about this fundraising event you mentioned on the phone, Grand-Mère," I said, taking a sip of my tea and savoring it. Grand-Mère's tea was unmatched; even I couldn't recreate it, and I'd watched her prepare it thousands of times.

"Oui. This Friday night. I think you'll find it appealing to your... creativity. Please come with me." She peered at me over her cup as she spoke.

I perked up. Creativity? "Is this an art auction for charity? I'd love to go!"

Grand-Mère nodded, taking a sip of her tea. "Something like that, *oui*. I'm so glad you'll attend. We'll have so much fun." She smiled and grasped my hand, giving it a gentle squeeze.

An art auction! I wished I had known about it sooner; I could've donated a piece to be auctioned off for charity. I made a mental note to find out when the next one would be so I could prepare something for it. My heart leapt thinking about what fun it would be to spend an evening pouring over the canvases, admiring them, and watching them bring in much-needed dollars for charity—which was?

"What charity is it for?"

"Save The Children Foundation. A worthy cause." Grand-Mère smiled at me, obviously pleased I was so interested in the event.

I grinned at her, taking a bite out of a cookie. "This is going to be a lot of fun, Grand-Mère. I'm looking forward to it."

Grand-Mère sat her teacup down. "Tell me, ma chère, what shall we wear to this event?" she asked with a mischievous grin.

CHAPTER 2

Ace

$\mathcal{M}$y alarm went off at 7 AM sharp on Monday morning, giving me just enough time to take a quick shower and head to my new "job." I was tempted to shut the alarm off, roll over, and sleep until noon as usual—pissing Dad off even more. But, seeing as how he'd made me hand over all the credit cards yesterday, I was at his mercy now.

"Fuck," I moaned, throwing back the covers and allowing the frigid morning air to hit my bare skin. This walking the straight and narrow bullshit was for the birds, but I figured if I played along for a few weeks and did things Dad's way, he'd come around. I'd get my plastic back, be able to quit this shitty job and get back to life as I had always known it.

We all knew Nick was the one who would end up running the company when Dad was gone, I thought as I made my way to the bathroom, rubbing my eyes and yawning. *Why make Jas and I jump through all these damned hoops?* I was getting angrier the more I thought about Dad and this stupid job he was making me take, and nothing good could come of that. I reminded myself it would only be for a few weeks. Probably.

I showered, dressed, grabbed some toast and coffee, and still made it to Dad's office by 8 AM. Okay, fine. 8:05 AM. He barely looked up from the stacks of paperwork on his desk as I strode into his spacious office. The room had a cozy feel to it with its oak desk and bookcases, a luxurious area rug, and the large leather couch and chairs. A bar filled with samples of Dalton Enterprises's whiskey, White Wolf, stood in one corner. Dad even smoked his cigars in here. He didn't give a damn that modern society generally frowned upon that these days.

I stood, waiting for an acknowledgment, hands clasped behind my back. I had even worn a black Armani suit I borrowed from Jasper, hoping to make a good impression. I figured the sooner I played nice and went along with this bullshit, the sooner Dad would give up and give my life back. Until then, it looked like I was a working man.

I cleared my throat. "So… I'm here," I finally said, after several awkward moments of silence.

"You're late." He glanced up at me for a split second, looking over the rim of his glasses, his bushy white eyebrows raised. He turned back to his paperwork with a scowl, signing page after page while continuing to ignore me.

I sighed. "Sorry. It won't happen again," I said, biting back the sarcastic retort on the tip of my tongue. Pissing Dad off immediately on my first day would not earn me any favors, I reminded myself.

Dad pressed a button on his desk phone, then continued signing papers while the monotone beep resonated. Finally, a woman's voice answered.

"Yes, Mr. Dalton?"

"Send Gregory in." No "please," no "thank you." And he wanted to bust Nick's balls for being a dick to everybody he came into contact with. The apple didn't fall far from the tree.

"Yes, sir."

I sighed again and shifted on my feet. *Bastard could at least invite me to sit down.*

After a couple of minutes, a man who looked about my age entered the office, shutting the door behind him. I could only assume this was Gregory. He was tall and lanky, with dusty brown hair, a thin face, and wire-rimmed glasses. He gave me a tentative smile as he moved to stand beside me in front of Dad's desk.

"Gregory, this is my son, Horace. He'll be your assistant." Dad barely looked up as he spoke. He shuffled some file folders to one side of his desk, opening one and continuing his task of signing papers.

I turned to Gregory and smiled. "Nice to meet you. Wow, I've never had an assistant before," I said with a little chuckle, looking from Gregory to Dad. Gregory's mouth tilted up on one side as he lowered his gaze, then looked to Dad.

"I meant YOU are HIS assistant, you fool," Dad bellowed. My face fell as I realized what was happening. Me? The son of the CEO, brother of the CEO in training... I was supposed to be some flunkie's assistant?

Gregory smiled apologetically as I looked back and forth between the two of them. "Wait. What?" Those two words were all I could manage. What the hell? Was he trying to embarrass me? Belittle me? Knock me down a notch or two? Well, mission fucking accomplished.

"You'll do whatever Gregory needs you to do. Now, go on," Dad said, effectively dismissing us. Gregory turned to go while I stood rooted to the spot, glaring at my father.

Dad looked up and met my scowl with one of his own.

"Have you got something to say to me, boy?"

Gregory stood, holding the door open for me. "If you'll follow me, Horace..." he said, trailing off, waiting awkwardly for me to end the staring contest with Dad.

My jaw clenched and my nostrils flared. I wanted to jump across that desk at Dad. I wanted to argue, scream, and call him names. But I didn't do any of those things. That would not get me back in his good graces and would not put a Dalton Enterprises credit card back in my wallet.

Instead, I scoffed and said, "No. No, it's all good." I turned on one foot and followed Gregory out of Dad's office. I couldn't help myself; I slammed the door as hard as I could behind me.

I stormed off down the hallway, not even sure where I was headed. I had no clue where Gregory's office was or if that's even where we were going, but I didn't care. I just needed to put some space between me and Dad. I heard Gregory's quickening footsteps behind me, trying to keep up.

"So, Horace, my office is actually in the other direction," he said, a little breathlessly.

A hot redhead in a black polka-dotted pencil skirt darted out of an office and into my path. I was so angry I couldn't even appreciate the way her ass rounded out that skirt right now.

"It's Ace, not Horace," I growled, ignoring his comment about his office's location. I stopped abruptly, making Gregory trip over his own feet to stop himself before plowing into me. I rubbed the back of my neck and closed my eyes. I had to play Dad's game. There was no other choice, I reminded myself.

"Okay... Ace. Look, I know this job isn't ideal for you. And I don't know what is going on between you and your father, but I can tell the situation is tense," he said slowly, choosing his words carefully.

I cut my eyes at him and nodded. I didn't trust myself not to take my frustrations out on this poor guy right now, so the less I said, the better.

He sighed. "I get the feeling this job is supposed to be some sort of punishment for you. But it doesn't have to be. Maybe it won't be so bad." A half-smile crept across Gregory's face as he shrugged and pushed his glasses up.

He was right. I was focusing on the wrong thing here — Dad. Since I had to be here, I should make the most of it. If the redhead was any indication, maybe there was some fun to be had in the office, after all. I could pretend to play his game, earn my paycheck, and liven things up around here. Just for a few weeks anyway, right? Dad would get tired of this bullshit game of his and fire me by then, I was sure. Mother would make him give my credit cards back, and all would be right in the world again.

I threw Gregory a half-cocked smile. "Alright, Greg. Lead the way, man."

THE REST OF THE DAY WENT BY IN A BORING BLUR. BUT Greg was turning out to be a decent guy and not some asshole boss. I called him Greg because "Gregory" made him sound like some old douchebag, in my opinion. We hung out in his office, talked a bit about sports and music, and had lunch together. When he had calls to take or actual work to do, I scrolled Facebook and watched TikTok videos on my phone. Not a bad first day, all in all. Turns out I was a great assistant. Screw you, Dad.

It was 5:00 PM, and I had just bolted out of Greg's office and was thinking I'd head to the nearest bar when I met Jasper in the hallway. I had avoided having my brothers bear witness to my public humiliation all day. Until now.

"How'd your first day go?" Jas asked, grabbing my shoulder. I shrugged him off and kept walking as he followed.

"Ask Dad," I said through gritted teeth. I continued through the maze of corridors, not even sure where the exit was at this point. Fuck, I needed to get out of here and get a drink, I thought as I took another wrong turn. And Jasper wasn't giving up. He tagged along right behind me.

"He actually just sent me to find you. He's requiring all of us to attend a charity event on Friday night. Wanted me to let you know it's part of your job now and to plan on being there," Jasper said apologetically. I stopped and turned to face him.

"For fuck's sake," I moaned, scrubbing my face with my hands. *Would someone wake me up from this goddamn nightmare already?*

"Relax, they're not so bad. Nick and I have to attend these things all the time. Free booze," he added, nudging my shoulder.

"I'm not going."

"You don't have a choice."

"Fuck." A couple of middle-aged women walked past just as I cursed, which drew their attention. One scowled at me, the other raised an eyebrow and looked me up and down with a smile playing on her lips.

Jasper shoved his hands in his pockets and sighed as he watched me eyeing the ladies as they walked by. I turned back to my brother. He wore a white button-down shirt with the sleeves rolled up to expose his forearms, his tie loosened around his neck, and a pair of navy pants that I'm guessing matched the suit jacket that was most likely hanging in his office right now. The very picture of the perfect son. Something I'd never be.

"Look. You're twenty-eight. You have to know it's about time to settle down. Dad's right. You're acting like a teenager... out drinking and gambling every night and fucking everything with a pulse. You don't have to become a straight-laced businessman; just take it down a few notches, dude," he said, ending in a low voice, which accentuated his southern drawl. I didn't look at him while he spoke, just kept my eyes on the asses of the two women as they disappeared down the hallway.

I knew he had a point. Hell, I even knew Dad had a point. I guess that's what pissed me off most, the fact that I didn't have this epiphany about my own life before he did. I didn't like it being forced on me. I knew things needed to change, but I should be allowed to change them in my own time and in my own way.

I didn't want to get into all of that deep shit with Jasper, though. Not now. I motioned to the exit door with a nod of my head, which I could now see was just around the corner to our left.

"Grab a drink with me?" I asked.

Jasper shook his head, a sad smile on his face. "Nah. Just make sure you're at the event on Friday, okay?" He patted my shoulder, then turned to walk back through the maze of hallways that was Dalton Enterprises.

THIRTY MINUTES LATER, I SAT AT THE BAR TWO BLOCKS from the office in downtown Nashville, enjoying my third shot of White Wolf while watching sports highlights on the big screen. Even though I had my issues with my family, Dad, in particular, I had to admit he made some damn fine whiskey. I swirled the golden liquid in the glass before downing it, trying not to think about Dad, Jasper, or Nick. Or what I was going to do now without Dad's goddamn money to finance my extracurricular activities. It was only a matter of time before some of my "acquaintances" started asking for more cash. I nodded to the bartender to bring me another shot, deciding I wouldn't think about it anymore today.

Instead, I took out my phone and pulled up the notepad app where I'd been writing a little lately. Maybe it was a song? Or a poem? Hell, I didn't know what to call it. But I'd heard that journaling helped clear the mind and relieve stress, so I thought I'd give it a try. Only what came out was in short lines and stanzas and possessed a rhythm and emotion that shocked even me.

An hour or so passed, then the after-work crowd started arriving at the bar. It was getting noisy, and I couldn't think, so I stopped writing and put my phone away. I checked my watch and decided maybe I'd better head home and try to get some sleep since I had to continue with this charade again tomorrow. I downed the last shot the bartender had sat in front of me and slapped a couple of bills on the bar to cover my tab. I noted my wallet growing thinner as I returned it to my pocket and grabbed my suit jacket, silently cursing my father.

THE REST OF THE WEEK WENT BY IN MUCH THE SAME WAY as my first day on the job. Avoiding my brothers, biting my tongue when it came to dealing with Dad, and doing as little as possible in my position as Greg's assistant. Greg didn't seem to mind that, which worked out great for me. I spent most of each workday on the phone with my contacts, getting in on some action with what little was left of my money. I bet a few dimes on the favorites in a couple of ball games; my cash was dwindling fast, and I knew my paychecks from Dalton Enterprises weren't gonna cut it. I had to do something.

Friday finally arrived, and Mother had made sure a "charity event" approved black Bottega Veneta tuxedo was hanging in my room. I sneered when I saw it, not looking forward to an evening of rubbing elbows with Nashville's elite. I was sure I'd manage to find some way to embarrass the family, either inadvertently or on purpose, which would bring another wave of Dad's wrath raining down on me at the next family meeting.

"No gettin' out of this," I told myself with a sigh. I pulled the tux off the hanger, resenting it and my family as I pulled it on and straightened my tie. *Just another damned hoop Dad is making me jump through.*

I stared at my reflection in the mirror briefly; not bad. Although I hated to admit it, I looked damn good in this tux. I'd tamed my blonde curls and my eyes shined back at me, bright ocean blue, in the reflection. My neck tattoo peeked out from the collar of my white shirt, a stark contrast to the businessman image Dad wanted me to project. I liked how it looked, though. I sighed. Too bad I'd be spending the evening at some stuffy charity event, bored beyond belief. *Free booze,* I reminded myself, and with one last glance, I headed out.

An hour later, I found myself in the Grand Lobby at The Union Station, elbow deep in Nashville socialites and business people. Dad held court at a large table, surrounded by other old men in tuxedos who were hanging on his every word. Occasionally, they all erupted into laughter at something the old man had said. He beamed, sitting there with a glass of whiskey in one hand, a cigar in the other, and my mother sitting right beside him, smiling primly and looking on.

Could someone remind me why the hell I am here again? My mood soured as I scowled, making my way to the open bar in one corner of the large lobby.

Jasper was nearby, nursing a drink and standing close to a pretty blonde, whispering in her ear while a coy smile spread across her face. I'd already witnessed Nick with a shapely redhead when I came in; she hung off his arm while he ignored her and craned his neck so he could hear whatever Dad was talking about to his business cronies. *Nobody mentioned I should bring a damn date to this thing.* I took my drink from the bartender and silently cursed my brothers.

I scanned the room after downing my whiskey. The place was packed. Women of all shapes and sizes in formal gowns, fake smiles plastered on their faces, and hair and makeup on point. I caught several of them ogling me, eye-fucking me even. *Maybe the night won't be a complete loss.* I winked back at one of them, causing her to blush and avert her eyes.

"Where's Horace?" I heard my father's voice boom from across the room. I took a deep breath and briefly closed my eyes before turning to find out what the old man wanted. Maybe I could fake a migraine and get out of here, I thought, managing a tight smile as I walked towards Dad's table.

A younger woman with a clipboard stood at his table, grinning and looking me up and down as I approached. She held her hand out to me and said, "Horace, it's so nice to meet you! Thank you so much for volunteering to help us out tonight. You are a lifesaver!" She offered a little giggle, looking from me to Dad. The others at the table laughed along with her. I stared blankly at her—Debbie, the little "hi, my name is" sticker attached to the front of her dress, read.

"Hi, Debbie, it's actually Ace. And I have no clue what you're talking about." I took her hand, squeezed quickly, and let go, still smiling awkwardly at her. Her brows knit together while her mouth formed a silent "oh."

"You'll be taking part in the auction tonight, Horace. It's for a good cause, didn't think you'd mind helping a worthy charity." Dad leaned back in his chair, a smug smile tugging at the corners of his mouth. He crossed his arms, observing me for a reaction.

I looked from Debbie to Dad, then Mother, who shrugged while cutting her eyes at Dad. "I'm sorry, I'm not following?" I asked, also crossing my arms, becoming a mirror image of my father. My gaze met his, and I could feel the tension between us thickening in the air.

Debbie cleared her throat, drawing our eyes to her. "Oh, it's a Bachelor Auction!" she crooned in her syrupy Southern accent, beaming at me. She placed one hand on my arm as she explained. "Don't you worry, it'll be fun! This is our first Bachelor Auction, and we're so happy you've decided to participate in it!"

I blinked several times in rapid succession as I looked at her. "What?" I asked after Debbie's words sunk in. Everyone was staring at me, some with smug grins, others with sympathetic eyes.

"You heard the woman, Horace. Being involved in charity work goes a long way in helping you climb the ladder at Dalton Enterprises, son. A long way, indeed," Dad said, taking a puff from his cigar, his gaze never leaving mine. I got the message, alright. I would have to take part in this fucking auction if I wanted to get any closer to getting my life back.

I clenched my jaw muscles, my nostrils flaring as I cut my eyes away from Dad. I'd be damned if I gave him the satisfaction of showing him how much this pissed me off. That's exactly what he wanted, but I wasn't taking the bait. *What the hell kind of game was the old bastard playing with me?* If it was games he wanted, games he would get. He had no idea who he was fucking with here.

I composed myself, turning my attention to Debbie, who looked like she'd been holding her breath while watching the silent exchange between Dad and me. The poor woman was probably on the verge of passing out when I said, "I'm happy to do it, Debbie. It warms my heart to help out the—" I stopped, looking around the lobby for a sign, a banner—anything—indicating what this goddamned charity event was for.

"Save the Children Foundation," Debbie supplied, raising her eyebrow and looking from me to Dad while holding her clipboard tight against her chest. Dad smirked, clearly entertained by watching me flounder for the charity's name.

"Exactly, Save the Children," I said, snapping my fingers with recognition. "There's nothing I wouldn't do for the children, Debbie." I took her hand, giving it a gentle squeeze while showing her a charming smile. Her face flushed as she took her hand back from mine, a slight grin forming on her lips.

"Well, Horace—Ace, I mean," she said, flustered and smiling shyly at me. "We are so happy to have you on board. I just know you're gonna raise a lot of money for the children tonight!" She beamed gratefully at me, giving me a once over and biting her lower lip before moving off to the next table, clipboard in hand.

The artificial smile immediately evaporated from my

face as I turned to Dad. I opened my mouth to speak, but he cut me off before I could say anything.

"Did you have something to add, Horace?" Dad asked, putting his cigar down and eyeing me from under his bushy white brows.

Of course I did. I wanted to tell him to take his money and go to hell. I wanted to say I didn't need him or his credit cards. I'd make my own way in the world. I wanted to throw something at him. Where the hell did he get off essentially whoring me out, even if it was for charity?

I wanted to say all of that, but I couldn't. I looked down at my Gucci shoes, my lips forming a tight line while my jaws clenched. This was a pissing contest, and Dad was showing me he had the biggest dick right now. He wanted to break me, make me bend to his will. And I didn't really have any other choice, now did I? Because without him and his money, what did I have?

With that grim realization, I looked up at my father. His hard eyes still focused on me, waiting for my reaction. I swept my gaze over all the faces sitting at Dad's table, all watching me. I could say something, but there would be no coming back, not if I embarrassed him in front of these assholes. So, I bit my tongue.

"Nope, nothing to say, Dad. Nothing at all." I took a drink from a passing server's tray and walked away.

Callie

GRAND-MÈRE AND I ARRIVED AT UNION STATION, WHERE the Save the Children Foundation was holding their fundraising event in the Grand Lobby, the centerpiece of the hotel. It was huge, with windows on all sides, a marble floor, crystal chandeliers, and intricate tiles on the large, arched ceiling. *Absolutely stunning*. The hotel itself was a work of art. I couldn't help but admire every detail as we entered the room.

I noticed several men staring at me as we made our way through the crowded room. I glanced down at myself; I wore a dark green gown with sequin accents and spaghetti straps. It showed some cleavage, but not too much. My long, dark brown hair was pulled up in a loose chignon at the base of my neck, and I wore dangly diamond earrings and a necklace to match. I took a deep breath and ignored the stares; I wasn't there looking for a date, anyway.

I followed my grandmother, who was also dressed to the nines, to a table where our names were on two placards, along with six others. She took a seat, gesturing for me to do the same, but I was itching to see the art. I looked around again, not seeing anything other than various people clad in black suits and formal gowns, milling around, laughing, and drinking.

"Grand-Mère, I'd like to find the art exhibits. Would you like to come with me?"

She pursed her lips, looking away. One lady seated at our table raised an eyebrow, looking from me to Grand-Mère.

"Ma chère, it's more of a… live presentation, shall we say? It will be later." She gestured again for me to sit, so I did. *A "live presentation" what the hell does that mean?*

A server brought around hors d'oeuvres and drinks, so I helped myself to some of each. I'd had two glasses of wine by the time people were finding their seats and the emcee began to speak. Grand-Mère cut her eyes at me, then smiled weakly.

A hush fell over the Grand Lobby as the lights dimmed

and everyone settled down. "Good evening, everyone! Welcome to the Save the Children Foundation's thirteenth annual fundraising event!" The emcee, an older man, dressed in a black tux with a red tie, waited for the applause to finish before continuing. "Tonight, we have an extra special event planned for you—something we've never done before!" Chuckles came from nearly every table while people nodded and smiled at one another.

A tiny ball of dread settled in my stomach as I looked around the room. Grand-Mère avoided my eyes, and the woman at our table who had looked confused at my mention of art exhibits earlier gave me an amused glance. Every table seemed to have a disproportionate number of females to males sitting around it. I swallowed hard, then turned my attention back to the emcee.

"Yes, folks. Tonight will be our first-ever Bachelor Auction! We have some of Nashville's most eligible men right here, waiting for you to win dates with them. I hope you've brought your wallets with you tonight, people; these guys are hot!" The emcee wiped his brow, then fanned himself as laughter erupted from the audience.

I turned my gaze on Grand-Mère, my eyes wide, my mouth hanging open. "A Bachelor Auction? Really?" I asked incredulously. This was the "art"? How could she bring me here under false pretenses? I had half a mind to grab my clutch and go right this minute, but her hand on my wrist stopped me.

"Caroline, it can't hurt, can it?" Grand-Mère asked, using my given name instead of the nickname she liked to call me. Her eyes pleaded with me, her hand clutching my arm. I closed my eyes briefly and shook my head. She released her grip on me, and I turned away from her, my mouth set in a firm line and my jaw clenched.

Fine, I'd stay. At least for now. But she hadn't heard the end of this.

"Before the bidding begins, let's meet our bachelors, shall we?" the emcee asked, grinning lasciviously. The audience cheered while I sat back in my chair with my arms crossed.

Ten men strode out onto the platform behind the emcee. Ten jaw-droppingly gorgeous men, I hated to admit. I averted my eyes and noticed Grand-Mère watching me.

"First, we have Braden Kennedy, a thirty-two-year-old banker from Brentwood! He is single and ready to mingle, ladies! Get your credit cards ready." The crowd tittered, and Braden smiled broadly, bowing exaggeratedly. Braden, although good-looking, was not my type; he was short. For me, that was a hard pass since I was five feet nine inches tall myself. I rolled my eyes when Grand-Mère caught my attention. She shrugged.

When the applause died down after the winner of his dates was announced, the emcee continued. "Next up, we have Ace Dalton! He's the twenty-eight-year-old middle son of Augustus Dalton, CEO of Dalton Enterprises. That whiskey you're drinking there, sir?" he asked a man seated at one of the tables up front. "It's 'White Wolf', produced by Dalton Enterprises!" The crowd applauded, some raising their tumblers of whiskey before downing them.

Ace. Ace. Why was that familiar? Then it came back to me. The bathroom at Indigo the night of Sarah's bachelorette party. There was an Ace and Michelle? Or maybe it was Becky? They were having sex in the bathroom.

I studied the man on the podium. Ace. That was not a common name. It had to be the same guy. He was tall, probably around six feet three inches. Muscular, but not bulky. Dark blond, curly hair on top, tapering to a close shave. Bright blue eyes, which looked cold and unfeeling at the moment. His broad shoulders were set and his hands clasped in front of him. I saw a tattoo on his neck, looked like a lotus flower from here, and more tattoos peeked out of the sleeves of his tux onto his hands as well. His mouth was pursed in a tight line as he gazed out into the crowd, almost as if he was looking past everyone. Smoking hot.

Definitely my type on paper.

The looks and even the bad boy attitude were right up my alley. But that was a place I didn't want to visit again. Not after Vic.

I caught Grand-Mère eyeing me, gauging my reaction to Ace. I silently mouthed, "No." She narrowed her eyes at me and cocked her head. I shook my head from side to side emphatically. She gave me a long look, and I knew what she was thinking.

She was going to bid on Ace for me.

I grabbed my clutch off the table and hurried out of the Grand Lobby as fast as I could.

Ace

I BIT THE INSIDE OF MY LIP, STARING OUT INTO THE crowd while the emcee talked about me as if I was cattle on the auction block instead of a person. A woman stood up from a table in the middle of the room and ran out the back; I wished I could follow her. I glanced at Dad, sitting with his cronies, with a smug look of satisfaction on his wrinkled, old face. Inspiration struck me at that moment. This was his idea, putting me on display, trying to embarrass me, or whatever the fuck his goal was. I decided to play along.

"Let's start the bidding now, shall we? How about one

thousand dollars... who will start the bidding at one thousand for three dates with Ace Dalton?" the emcee asked, motioning at me with one hand while holding the mic with the other. I saw many bidding paddles rise into the air, some higher than others and some being waved around with enthusiasm.

Let's raise some goddamn money, then.

I caught the eye of a pretty redhead at a table up front. I winked at her and bit my lip. Her face flushed as she smiled and raised her paddle in the air.

"Oh boy, the competition is fierce for this one! Let's go ahead and up the ante. How about five thousand?" the host asked, raising an eyebrow and looking out into the audience. Several paddles went down, but more than a few stayed in the air. I popped my collar and struck a pose, shooting a sly grin out into the sea of faces staring at me. Dad cocked his head to the side, narrowing his eyes at me. I ignored him and decided to really put on a show. Isn't this what he wanted? I gyrated my hips to the background music, which brought shrieks and laughter from the audience.

"Seven thousand!" a female voice cried from the audience.

"Eight!" another woman yelled, waving her paddle in the air.

"Eight thousand dollars, wowsa! Anyone willing to go higher? Remember, you'll get not one, not two, but three dates with this hot fella!" the emcee reminded everyone. I kept my show going, making eye contact and smiling with as many women as I could. My gaze roamed over the crowd, and I spotted an elderly woman with graying brown hair, holding a paddle in the air.

Oh, come on. If I have to be auctioned off like a piece of meat, at least let one of these hot chicks win, for the love of God. I wasn't sure He was listening right now, though, or else I probably wouldn't have been in this situation to begin with.

"Nine thousand, going once, going twice..." the emcee called out, looking incredibly pleased.

At the last moment, the old woman jumped up with her paddle. "Ten thousand!"

The last two or three remaining paddles went down. Gasps filled the air as everyone turned to look at her. She smiled triumphantly as the emcee pointed at her.

"Ten thousand dollars! Going once... going twice... SOLD to the lady in the blue dress! The children thank you for your support, enjoy your dates with Mr. Dalton!" he announced to cheers and applause. I caught Dad clapping and smirking at me. My brothers were laughing as well.

Fuck this shit.

I stomped off the stage and headed directly to the bar, pulling my tie loose as I went.

Callie

I STOOD ON THE CURB IN FRONT OF UNION STATION, waiting for the Uber I'd ordered. I couldn't believe Grand-Mère would do this to me. I felt like a fool for thinking she had given up the husband search. I should've known better. That part was on me. I let my guard down, but it wouldn't happen again. If she'd just spent thousands of dollars on a date with Ace Dalton on my behalf, then she'd wasted her money. No way in hell would I go out with him.

Feeling exhausted suddenly, I spotted a bench nearby. I collapsed onto it, putting my head in my hands. Why did this damn trust have to have such a stupid condition on it? Why would my parents do this to me? Why wouldn't Grand-Mère let me live my own life? If I forfeited the trust and made my own way, what was so wrong with that? The questions invaded my thoughts, overwhelming me until I felt tears streaming down my cheeks.

I'd just have to sit her down and talk to her. Make her understand once and for all that I wouldn't force this. If I happened to meet someone in the next two years and happened to get married, then great. But I would not marry someone simply for money. I couldn't do it.

I composed myself, drying my tears with the back of my hands. *Where the hell is my Uber?*

I looked up to see Ace stumbling out of the hotel entrance, cigarette in his mouth, his tie loosened, and the top few buttons of his shirt undone. He'd discarded the jacket, and his sleeves were rolled up, exposing even more tattoos on his muscular forearms. He looked pissed, which intrigued me. Maybe he wasn't happy about this auction either, though I couldn't imagine why a guy like him wouldn't be. I watched as he took a draw from his cigarette, leaving it dangling from his lips while he took his cell phone out from his pocket. After a moment of scrolling and tapping the screen, he put it to his ear and paced the side-walk in front of the Station.

As I watched him, I wondered if she'd done it. *Stop, Callie. It doesn't matter if she did it or not. You're not going out with him.* I watched him pace while talking on the phone. His tattoos were amazing, mesmerizing, even. If his thick fore-arms were any indication of what else was hidden under those clothes… I shook my head. *Stop.*

He scowled, taking the cigarette from his lips, letting a cloud of smoke bloom as he exhaled. I couldn't take my eyes off him, and I hated it. Ace Dalton was sexy as hell and completely my type. He had it all, and that's exactly why I couldn't have him. Vic had made sure I'd never go down that path again. What I needed was a nice accountant, or maybe someone like Braden Kennedy, the short banker who was on the auction block earlier. Someone who played by the rules and wouldn't hurt me. That was not and never would be Ace.

He paced closer and closer to me, and I cursed my Uber driver for not being here already. Ace met my gaze and raised an eyebrow, giving me a small smile before the scowl returned. My insides turned into molten lava immediately; I turned away, hoping he didn't see me blush. *Damn it, Callie.*

"I heard you, Andre. I'll get you the money, don't worry about it." He continued to pace, taking another draw from his cigarette. Other people were filing out of the Station now; the auction must be on intermission. All the more reason why my Uber needed to show up. I didn't want Grand-Mère coming out here looking for me.

"You know I'm good for it. Fuck what you heard, man."

I couldn't help but listen. Sounded like trouble. *None of your business.*

"Yeah, okay." He punched the screen and shoved the phone into his pocket, stopping only a few feet from where I sat on the bench.

"Fuck." He ran one hand through his hair, then noticed me sitting there, trying to pretend I wasn't watching or listening to him. *Fuck, indeed.*

"Sorry," he said, one side of his mouth quirking up as he shrugged.

I shrugged back. "No worries." I looked past him, hoping to see my Uber coming for me, but no such luck. The molten lava had coursed through my veins now, and I needed to get away from him.

To my utter horror, he sat down on the opposite end of

the bench and took a last drag from his cigarette. He put it out against the bottom of his shoe and flicked it at a nearby trash can, impressively making it in. He put his head in his hands and sighed.

I pursed my lips and looked at him, then looked around. People were heading back inside now. I wasn't sure if I should say something or not. I mean, I didn't know him. I didn't want to know him, either. But he seemed to be hurting or in trouble, at least. Like a wounded predator — a wolf, maybe. I could try to help, but I might get bitten in the process.

"So, ummm. Are you okay?" I winced. *So stupid*.

He looked up at me, his eyes softening. "Yeah, thanks."

I nodded, looking away. *Okay, I've done my good deed. He's fine*.

"It's just hard when people expect shit from you that you're not capable of, you know?"

I whipped my head back towards him, not sure he was talking to me. He made eye contact briefly. Then it was his turn to look away. Butterflies took flight amid the molten lava in my stomach.

"Actually, yeah. I do know." Did those words come out of my mouth? Apparently, they did.

Our eyes met again, his blazing like blue flames, sparking something inside of me I needed to keep hidden in the dark. Fear sliced through my heart just as I heard a car horn beep. *My Uber, finally. Thank God*.

I took a deep breath, breaking eye contact. "Well. Bye." I moved as quickly as my dress would allow and got into the car. I couldn't help but glance at him as he watched the car drive away, a hint of a smile playing on his lips.

He's not the man for you, Callie. I closed my eyes and leaned my head against the window as the car sped away, pushing all thoughts of Ace Dalton out of my brain.

CHAPTER 3

Ace

I sat in Greg's office, bouncing a Nerf ball off the wall while he talked on the phone. He glanced at me a couple of times with a frown, but I was oblivious to anything but my thoughts. I couldn't get her out of my head, and I didn't even know her name.

I ran through the night of the charity event in my head again, for about the hundredth time. This gorgeous woman had been sitting on a bench in front of Union Station by herself. I knew she'd been attending the fundraiser because of the formal gown she wore and I couldn't help but notice how it hugged every curve of her perfect body. She looked sad, like she'd been crying. I wondered why and felt an irrational urge to punch whoever had made her feel that way.

I'd been on the phone with Andre, who had informed me that my card had been declined and I was still on the hook for twenty grand, thanks to Dad, when I spotted her. As fucked up as it sounded, I was drawn to her and couldn't help sitting down on the bench next to her.

When she had asked if I was okay, being obviously upset herself, my icy heart melted just a little. Before I knew it, I was saying some stupid shit about not being able to live up to other people's expectations. She'd surprised me by saying she knew how I felt.

Then she was gone.

And I didn't even get her name.

I tossed the ball at the wall again, harder this time. So many women in this city, and I could have damn near any of them. But not her. I'd probably never even see her again.

"Ace, please," Greg whispered, covering the mouthpiece of his phone. He gave me an apologetic look, then went back to his call. I tossed the ball on the floor and ran my hands through my hair. I sighed. I'd just have to forget about her and concentrate on the problem at hand—getting out of the three dates with the old lady who bought my ass at the auction.

I stood, motioning to Greg that I was leaving, and he waved me off with a scowl. I headed towards Dad's office. There had to be something he could do to get me out of this. No matter how badly he wanted to put me in my place, this was over the line.

I saw him through the window of his office, talking animatedly on the phone. I couldn't make out his words, but his voice was loud. Nick sat in one of the wingback guest chairs in front of Dad's desk, his hands steepled beneath his chin and a scowl on his face. Dad slammed the phone down, and I saw the vein in his forehead pulsing. He looked up just then and caught my eye, then, with a nod of his head, motioned for me to come in.

I opened the door cautiously. I wished I had waited until tomorrow to talk to Dad, but it was too late now. I entered his office, closing the door behind me and taking the chair next to Nick without a word.

"Goddamn it!" My father picked up a paperweight from his desk and hurled it across the room, where it put a damn good dent in the wall before hitting the floor. I blinked a few times, cutting my eyes back and forth between the old man and Nick.

"We'll fix it, Dad. They don't have a leg to stand on," Nick said calmly. He leaned back in his chair, rubbing his eyes. Now that I took a closer look at the two of them, they appeared haggard and stressed out. Both of them looked sleep-deprived and had bags underneath their eyes.

"What's going on?" I asked, unable to stop myself. The two of them exchanged a look as if silently agreeing to tell me the truth.

"We're being sued. Class action lawsuit, as a matter of fact. And we've been ordered to cease and desist manufacturing until further notice." Nick rubbed his temples as he explained.

My mouth dropped open. "What? Why?" It was no secret; I knew nothing about this business of distilling whiskey. I had a feeling I was about to learn, though.

Dad sighed. "It's a fungus. Baudoinia. Forms when the ethanol evaporates from the whiskey during the maturation process." He shook his head, his jowls waggling and his bushy eyebrows raised.

"The Angel's Share," I supplied. I was proud I actually knew something about the process, although most people had probably heard of this before.

Dad nodded. "That's right. This fungus, naturally occurring, mind you, feeds on the ethanol and spreads. It's not new. It's been around for centuries," he explained with a huff.

"It causes black, sooty gunk to appear on everything. You've probably seen it and didn't even know what you

45

were looking at," Nick added. He sighed heavily and looked at Dad.

"Yeah, I've seen it. So, why the lawsuit?"

"The Environmental Council has taken it upon themselves to blame us for this visual blight on Nashville's buildings and tourist attractions. Although the fungus has been around longer than any of us have walked on this planet," Dad said bitterly. His intercom beeped. He punched the button and growled, "No more calls today, Sherry."

I was trying to connect the dots but was having some trouble. My brows knit together as I thought. "So, how can they order you to cease and desist if this stuff has been around forever, anyway?"

"Good question, son. One that my lawyers are going to answer as soon as possible." Dad picked up the phone again and asked Sherry to get a buddy of his on the phone, Kenneth, who was a big shot lawyer here in town.

"The Council has some pull now that they've gotten some heavy hitters to back them. They've got some big names with a lot of money on their side now, so they're getting more attention and being taken seriously. It's bad news, Ace." Nick gave me a somber look and sighed.

"What can we do?" I asked. I was genuinely concerned and also shocked that I gave a damn.

Dad hung up the phone just then after securing an appointment with his lawyer friend and turned his attention to me. "We will handle it. It's none of your concern. Just continue doing whatever Gregory has you doing."

That couldn't have stung more if he had physically slapped my face. I clenched my jaw, looking from one to the other of them. "So, you're making me work here to teach me some responsibility, but I'm not good enough to handle the real stuff. Is that what you're saying? You've got me playing around with Greg, doing bullshit work, to teach me a lesson. You don't trust me to do any actual work?"

Dad shook his head. "Son, this is way over your head."

I nodded, smiling ruefully. "I get it."

Just the way I got it in high school when I chose not to go out for the football team, and Dad expressed his utter disappointment in me. And how I got it when I tried out for the baseball team to make him happy and didn't make it. His disdain for me grew even more. And I got it when I heard him talking to Mother about how I wasn't like Nick or Jasper—sports wasn't my thing. I was the black sheep, the disappointment in the family. So, when I decided to live up to that reputation, it deepened the rift between us even further. When I snuck out late at night, got arrested for underage drinking, accumulated DUIs after I got my license, and totaled my first car, it only cemented Dad's opinion of me.

Immature. Irresponsible. Reckless.

That was me, Ace Dalton, in my father's eyes.

I stood, nodding to Nick, before heading for the door. If they wanted to handle this on their own, fine by me. I didn't give a shit about the company, anyway; all I wanted was to get my credit cards back and get the hell out of this bullshit job. I couldn't believe I entertained the idea of trying to help them in the first place.

"If you need me, I'll be in Greg's office," I said before slamming the door behind me.

Callie

I TOSSED A TUBE OF COBALT BLUE ONTO MY DESK WITH A sigh. I glared at the commissioned painting I was working on—correction, trying to work on. I couldn't get my mind off the bachelor auction long enough to concentrate on my work.

I hadn't spoken to Grand-Mère since that night, but not for lack of her trying. She'd called every day, and I had let it go to voicemail and hadn't bothered to listen to her messages. I nearly stabbed the canvas with my paintbrush just thinking about it.

It was tempting to at least listen to her messages. I was curious… did she buy the dates with Ace or not? *It doesn't matter, Callie.* I had to keep telling myself that because the memory of Ace sitting on that bench beside me, his deep-voiced drawl, made me flush every time I thought about it.

Deciding to stop work on the client's painting for the day before I accidentally ruined it, I set about putting my paints away and washing my brushes. I was in the kitchen, laying them out on a towel to dry, when I heard a knock at the door. I wasn't expecting anyone and thought about not answering it. *Probably just a package delivery, anyway.* I shrugged, deciding I'd better see who it was. I dried my hands on my paint-splattered shirt and went to answer the door.

I flung the door open to reveal Grand-Mère standing there with a plate of madeleines covered with saran wrap in her hands. I should've known it was her. I berated myself for answering the door. I started to close it without a word, but she put a bony hand on the door frame to stop me.

"Caroline. Ma chère, I know you're upset with me. Please, can we talk about it?" Her face was pale, and her wrinkles seemed much more pronounced than I remembered. She probably hadn't been eating or sleeping. Part of me was glad she was miserable because she kind of

48

deserved it after what she pulled. It alarmed the other part of me to see her this way. She was my Grand-Mère, after all, the woman who raised me since I was twelve years old. I sighed and opened the door wider to allow her in.

"*Merci,*" she said, sliding past me and into my living room. She placed the plate of madeleines on my coffee table; she knew it was my favorite treat. I resisted the urge to dig in. They would just have to wait.

I stood looking at her as she sat down on the couch. I put my hands on my hips and took a deep breath. "Okay. You want to talk, let's talk. Why would you pull a stunt like that, Grand-Mère?"

She folded her hands in her lap, looking up at me. "Caroline, I know how much Vic hurt you. But that doesn't mean you should shun love forever." I began shaking my head, but she continued. "There are still good ones out there, ma chère. You deserve to find love, whether or not there's a trust deadline."

I felt my resolve weakening when she put it like that; she sensed it too.

"I saw the way you looked at Ace. I had to do it."

I whipped my head towards her, meeting her eyes.

"You won the dates with him?"

She smiled slyly, enjoying this. "I did."

She won the dates with Ace. For me.

"How much?" I asked, crossing my arms.

Grand-Mère raised an eyebrow. "It's my gift to you. Don't worry about the cost."

But I did worry. I knew she had some money put back from when Grand-Père had passed away, but she shouldn't have used it for something like this. It was crazy. I sighed. Just another reason I needed to inherit the damn trust.

She held a hand out to me, inviting me to sit with her, so

I did. She wrapped an arm around me, pulling me close, resting her chin on top of my head.

"Vic mistreated you. I know that. He was an alcoholic, he cheated on you repeatedly, he abused you with his words. I know all of it. If I could get my hands on him right now, I would kill him for it." She pulled back, taking my face in her hands, looking me in the eye.

"Don't let what happened with him keep you from finding love. Real love, this time. It exists, ma chère. And you deserve it." She planted a kiss on my forehead. I felt tears pricking my eyes, threatening to fall.

"And yes, it would be nice for you to inherit your trust. That's been my goal, to help you do just that so you can be free to do what you want with your life. Traveling the world with someone you love, painting everything you see. But most of all, I want you to love and to be loved, Caroline."

That did it. The tears fell freely now. I wrapped my arms around her waist and sobbed into her blouse while she stroked my back. I had no idea. I thought it was all about the money, all this time. How could I have thought that?

"Thank you, Grand-Mère," I choked out through the tears.

She was right. I knew she was right. I remembered the years I'd spent with Vic, how much I'd loved him despite everything he did to me. I'd met him in college, but he dropped out after only a few months. He was my type on paper, everything I was drawn to—tattoos, muscles, he even had a motorcycle. Bad boy, inside and out. I couldn't resist him, and being with him was amazing in the beginning. We went for long rides on his bike and he introduced me to his friends. The sex was mind-blowing. Before I knew it, we were living together.

That's when things changed.

He started going out without me, staying out all night

sometimes, coming home drunk off his ass. He'd get mad when I questioned him about it. He said my art was a waste of time, that I should get a real job and earn more money. Meanwhile, he could barely stay employed, getting fired from one job after another.

We fought constantly. He didn't even bother to try hiding the other women anymore towards the end. I blamed myself for not being enough for him. I made excuses for his behavior. And I kept on loving him, even though he didn't deserve it.

I kept loving him until I didn't love me anymore. And that's when I knew it was over.

I left one night while he was out, taking only my essential belongings with me. I changed my phone number, and I stayed with Sarah for a while. Eventually, he found out where I was. He tried to convince me to come back, said he had changed and that he was sorry. That he loved me.

But if that's what love was, I didn't want it.

I'd stayed single ever since I left Vic, too afraid to go down that road again. I knew Grand-Mère was right; not every man was like Vic. I just didn't know if I could put my heart on the line again, though.

"So, will you give it a chance? Go out with Ace?" she asked, hope in her voice.

I could go on one date. *One date couldn't hurt, right?* It would make her happy, and I could say I at least tried. I just wouldn't go on the other two dates with him. I'd make up an excuse. One date, that's all. Besides, maybe he wouldn't even like me, which would be the end of it anyway.

One date.

"Yes, Grand-Mère. I'll go out with Ace."

Ace

I sat at the bar, whiskey in one hand and my phone in the other, my notepad app pulled up. It was getting pretty late, and I'd been here for a while; I'd come straight over from work, which was about two blocks from here. I needed to think, and what usually helped me do that was a drink and some time spent writing.

Fear, passion, glory
Stirring his flesh and bones
With one look from her
To feed his fading flame

It had taken me an hour to write that much, and it was shit. I couldn't focus my thoughts; there were too many of them. And the most pressing one was how to get out of these goddamned dates with the old lady who had won the bachelor auction. I'd had a message earlier from someone called Cindy from Save the Children, with a perky, sweet-sounding southern twang in her voice. Just calling to let me know that Ms. Harrison would like to schedule her first date with me as soon as possible. Fuck.

The whole thing was ridiculous. I needed to talk to Dad first thing tomorrow, get him to reimburse the old woman the $10k she'd spent on the dates. He should never have signed me up for that bullshit in the first place without asking me.

But catching Dad alone and in the mood to talk the last few days had been impossible. The cease and desist order and the impending lawsuit had him in meeting after meeting, or on the phone, yelling at someone or other. And if he wasn't doing either of those things, then Nick and Jasper were with him in his office, pouring over documents until late into the evening. I hadn't had a second alone with Dad to plead my case, much less express my displeasure at being put in this situation to begin with.

I sighed. I'd just have to call Cindy back myself tomorrow and tell her I'm not doing it. Tell her to send an invoice to Dad for the $10k and let the chips fall where they may.

It was getting late, and I was getting nowhere with this poem, anyway. I needed a smoke, so I figured it was time to head home. I laid a twenty-dollar bill on the table, shoved my phone into my pocket, then headed out.

I walked towards the parking garage where I'd left my Jeep. Broadway was still pretty busy with people pouring in and out of the bars, walking up and down the sidewalks. I turned down an alley that led to the garage behind the bar. It was dark, but I could see my bright red Jeep up ahead. It hardly ever got really cold in Nashville, but the air had a crisp chill in it tonight.

OOOOOFFFF. I doubled over, holding my stomach where a fist had just landed in my gut, knocking the wind out of me.

"What the fuck?" I asked, looking up to see two shadowy figures blocking my way.

"Dalton?" one of them asked, flexing his hand. As my eyes adjusted to the dim lighting, I could see them better. Both of them were massive, with arms as big as tree trunks, and they were at least as tall as I was.

I winced as I stood up straight. "Who wants to know?" A lead ball settled in the pit of my stomach; I had a feeling I knew exactly who had sent these guys.

"We're from the Collection Agency. Just a friendly reminder, you have an unpaid bill in the amount of $20k. You've got ten days to pay up, or we'll settle up another way. Got it?" The big guy on the right cocked his head at me, waiting for an acknowledgment.

Fuck.

I looked from one to the other of them, making contact with their steely eyes. *Shit*. How the hell was I going to get my hands on twenty grand in the next ten days? I took a few moments too long for their taste; the big guy on the left made a move towards me. I held up a hand, nodding my head.

"Got it, I've got it, okay?" The guy stopped in his tracks, looked at the other one, who nodded his head. They turned, disappearing into the shadows of the parking garage, and before I knew it, they were gone. As if they'd never even been there.

If not for the pain in my stomach, I'd have thought I imagined the whole thing.

I slowly made my way to the Jeep. I fumbled with my keys, finally got in, and slammed the door a little too hard. Then I punched the steering wheel.

"FUCK!" I yelled into the void. A faint echo yelled back at me from the nearly empty garage.

No way was Dad going to spring for paying ten thousand to get me out of those dates and pay off my debt to Andre. I didn't know how, but I was going to have to convince Dad to pay Andre. The dates with the old lady were nothing compared to what I could expect from the "Collection Agency" if I didn't pay up. I closed my eyes, letting my head fall back against the headrest. I could see Dad's smug grin now, the knowledge that he'd been right about me all along, glinting in his eyes. I didn't want to ask him for the money, but what other choice did I have?

Twenty. Thousand. Dollars.

Ten. Days.

Maybe I'd talk to Jasper about it first. Maybe my kid

brother had some cash he could loan me. I immediately felt guilty for even thinking about asking Jas for money. What the fuck was I going to do?

I took a deep breath, slamming my palm against the steering wheel again. Ten days. I had to put Dad's game into overdrive, and I had exactly ten days to make him see I was completely on board with his plan to get my shit together. I'd convince him to give my credit cards back. I had to.

Bitching to him about the auction was out. I had to play along, show him I could man up and that I could be trusted. Could I do it in ten days, though? I had no choice but to try.

I guess that meant I had a date with Ms. Harrison to arrange.

CHAPTER 4

Callie

I sat at the bar in a fancy restaurant on 4th Avenue, nursing a glass of wine while I waited for Ace to show up. It was a cozy, upscale joint that required reservations, which I'd made a few days in advance. I wore a short black cocktail dress with heels; I figured since Ace was so tall, I didn't have to worry about heels making me taller than my date like I normally did. My long brown hair fell in beachy waves over my shoulders, and I'd even put on fake lashes for this. I wished I had time to go to the bathroom to give my hair and makeup one final look, but he was due to arrive any minute now.

I'd asked the girl, Cindy, from Save the Children, to have Ace meet me here instead of picking me up. It made me feel better knowing my own car was right outside if I felt the need to leave. Who knew how this was going to go, so it was better to be safe than sorry. I glanced at the time on my phone again. A whole kaleidoscope of butterflies took flight in my stomach, sending a wave of nausea over me.

What am I doing? I took a deep breath. *I'm giving this a chance. For Grand-Mère, that's what I'm doing.* I repeated that, over and over, until the overwhelming urge to throw up subsided. Just when the butterflies had settled down, the door opened, and there he was.

Ace Dalton, looking sexy as hell.

There went those butterflies again.

He stopped just inside the doorway to look around. A white dress shirt hung loosely from his broad shoulders, the sleeves rolled up to reveal his tattooed forearms. Black pants hugged his narrow waist. An expensive-looking silver watch adorned his wrist, along with a few silver rings on his fingers. His blonde curls were slightly unruly, and there was a bit of stubble on his jaw and chin.

Completely my type on paper. *Keep your guard up, Callie.*

I took a deep breath as I saw him approach the host. After a moment, the host gestured in my direction at the bar, Ace's gaze following. Our eyes locked, and I saw recognition and delight on his face as a small smile tugged at his lips. He began making his way towards me, his smoldering eyes never leaving mine. I swallowed hard as he neared.

He stopped in front of me and cocked his head to one side while a half-smile appeared on his face. "It's you. From the bench at Union Station."

"It's me," I agreed with a shy smile of my own.

"Not the Ms. Harrison I was expecting, but I'm not mad about it." His gaze swept over me appreciatively as he held out his hand. Without a word, I took it, and he raised my hand to his lips, brushing a gentle kiss over my knuckles while still holding my gaze. I felt my soul leave my body momentarily before I found my voice again.

"You thought my grandmother won the dates for herself?" I couldn't help but grin, picturing it. What a laugh she would get out of that when I told her about it later.

He grinned shyly, glancing at the floor before looking up again. "I did. I'm happy to find that I was wrong."

Blood rushed to my face, and I bit the inside of my lip to suppress a giddy smile. *Stop it.*

Suddenly, he shook his head and ran one hand through his hair. "Sorry. Ace Dalton. And your first name, Ms. Harrison?"

"Caroline. Everyone calls me Callie, though."

The corners of his mouth turned up as he studied me. "Callie. That's perfect."

He had looks and charm. It was not going to be easy to keep my guard up, but I had to try. I looked away, pursing my lips, and saw the host heading in our direction.

"Harrison? Party of two? Your table is ready now; please follow me."

Ace extended one arm to indicate I should go first. I trailed behind the host, weaving between tables until we arrived at a small table for two in a secluded back corner of the restaurant.

"Enjoy," the host said, leaving us alone at the dimly lit table.

"We definitely will," Ace said, with a panty-melting grin as we sat down.

Do not let yourself be fooled, Callie. Remember the bathroom at Indigo? Michelle/Becky? That's the kind of guy he is, so don't start thinking this can be anything other than what it is, an arranged date. Just one date, that's all it'll ever be.

I gathered my resolve like a cloak around myself as I met his gaze, recalling the night at Indigo and how he'd been fucking a girl whose name he didn't even know in the restroom. I also remembered Grand-Mère's words. *"Don't let what happened with Vic keep you from finding love."* But I smothered that little voice before it could rip my determination away.

"So, have you been here before?" Ace asked, picking up a menu. I did the same, flipping a menu open, becoming engrossed in reading the descriptions of the salads.

"Only once. A long time ago. You?" I asked, deliberately keeping my response short.

I noticed his brow crease as he glanced at me over the top of his menu. "A few times."

I nodded, taking a sip from one of the glasses of water that had been waiting at the table for us.

"I think I'll have the Filet Mignon," he murmured, still looking at the menu. When I didn't say anything back, he sighed, closed the menu, and laid it on the table.

"Did I miss something during the walk from the bar to the table, Callie?"

I acted taken aback. "What do you mean?"

He raised an eyebrow. "Call me crazy, but I sensed a mutual attraction between us back there at the bar. Now I'm sensing an ice-cold wall. What's going on?"

I sighed, laying my menu on the table as well. "Ace, we both know this whole thing is ridiculous. My grandmother won a few dates with you, and now you're obligated to go out with me. Don't worry, I'm not holding you to the remaining two dates." I bit my lip and looked up at him. He frowned, his blue eyes darkening.

"Okay. So, you're just here for the one date to make your grandmother happy, is that it?"

I rolled my eyes, then looked down at my lap where my fingers were absently folding and unfolding the hem of my cocktail dress. "I mean, yeah. I'm sure you don't really want to be here. Right?"

He nodded and smiled, but there seemed to be a sadness

attached to it now. "I get it, yeah. Your grandmother won the dates for you; you probably didn't even want to do this."

What the hell am I doing? Ruining this, that's what. But I couldn't stop myself.

I plastered a tight smile on my face. "Right."

Ace

I LEANED BACK IN MY CHAIR AFTER FINISHING MY STEAK, watching Callie as she moved the croutons in her salad back and forth, pretending to eat. We hadn't said much since the food arrived, and frankly, I was confused and a little pissed off.

I knew she was attracted to me. I saw it in her eyes, back at the bar. She was obviously doing her best to talk herself out of it, though, and I had no idea why. Was it my reputation? In my experience, my status as one of Nashville's most notorious playboys rarely scared women off—it usually made them even bolder in approaching me. But, as I watched her ignoring me, playing with the food on her plate, I realized that Callie wasn't like those women.

I also realized I liked that about her.

I had to figure this out before the end of the night if I wanted a chance at another date with her. I wadded up the linen napkin I'd just used to wipe my mouth and laid it on the table beside my plate, leveling my eyes at the beautiful brunette before me.

"So, why would your grandmother spend $10k on three dates with me that you didn't even want in the first place?"

She met my eyes, hers wide as saucers, startled with the blunt question I asked. She furrowed her brow and laid the fork down, giving up on the pretense of eating her meal. "I don't know. You'd have to ask her."

"Bullshit. Tell me."

She scoffed and looked away, glancing around the dining room as if someone could rescue her. Finally, she sighed and narrowed her eyes at me. "Fine. If you really want to know, she's eager for me to find someone to get serious with and settle down. Get married."

Now we were getting somewhere. I continued, treading carefully, now that I had her talking. "Aren't there easier ways to find a boyfriend besides spending thousands of dollars at a bachelor auction? Dating apps, for example?"

She rolled her eyes at me. "Yeah, well, we've been through all of that already. And I'm stubborn." She quirked her lips up on one side in amusement, glancing at me for a reaction.

I grinned. "Okay, so this was a last resort. What's the big hurry?"

Her smile faltered, and I almost thought I'd lost her. She looked down at her lap, then propped one elbow on the table and put her chin in her hand. "My parents died when I was twelve. They left my inheritance in a trust, but the catch is that I can't inherit it until I'm thirty. And I have to be married."

I winced at hearing that. "Harsh."

"Yeah. I mean, I'm twenty-eight, and I don't feel ready to get serious with anyone, much less start thinking about marriage. I don't care about the money, honestly, but Grand-Mère is dead set on it. She wants me to be free to travel and work on my art, and the money would allow me to do that. I'm torn, you know? I want to make her happy, but at the same time, I want to make me happy, too. Does that even make sense?"

I watched as she spoke, the words coming out of her

like a tidal wave once she got started. God, she was beautiful. Those dark blue eyes of hers, in contrast with her fair skin and mahogany hair, were incredible. I felt a smile tugging at my lips while she explained her predicament, waving her hands in the air as she talked. She was unlike anyone I'd ever met before, and it was refreshing. An artist? Who knew, but I could see it. She seemed like a creative type. She had decided to open up to me, and I couldn't have been happier about it.

When she was done, she sat staring at me, waiting for a response. And for whatever reason, I found myself blurting out, "Yeah, it makes perfect sense, actually. I sort of have the same problem with my father." *Why the fuck would I bring that up?*

"You do?" she asked, looking a little relieved, prompting me to go on. So, I did.

"Yeah. I mean, I have a bit of a reputation," I said, pausing when I saw her trying to suppress a laugh. "I know, I know. I'm not real proud of myself, okay?" It surprised me to hear those words coming out of my mouth, but there they were. She was listening raptly, hanging on to every word, so I continued.

"He thinks it's time I settled down, so he cut me off financially and made me start working at the family business. He's trying to teach me a lesson by bringing me down a few notches. And the thing that pisses me off most is that I know he's right. I just don't like being forced into things."

She nodded, taking a sip from her glass of wine. "That's fair."

"I have some... issues... I need to take care of, and to do that, I have to play along with his game. Make him see that I'm on board and hope that he buys it in time." I stopped talking, realizing I may have said too much.

"In time?" Callie asked.

63

I waved her off. "It doesn't matter. Anyway, I get where you're coming from. I do."

She sat her wineglass down and cocked her head at me, smiling. "You know, it's nice to talk to someone who understands. I don't really have anyone else who does. My best friend, Sarah, is about to get married, and all my other friends are already married, having babies, or have thrown themselves into their careers." She paused as if thinking about something, then hesitantly reached across the table, putting her hand on mine. "Thank you, Ace."

It was as if until this very moment, I hadn't truly been alive. My life had been in black and white, and suddenly, I was seeing it in technicolor. There was a spark of light in the cold, dark recesses of my heart for the first time in — well, ever. The touch of her hand on mine sent a bolt of electricity through me, jolting me to life when I didn't even know I'd been a dead man all this time.

"Welcome," I managed to say. She withdrew her hand from mine, leaving me feeling cold almost immediately. As of this moment, I had a new goal in life, and it involved having Callie Harrison's hands on me again soon. I didn't know how or when, but it had to happen.

CHAPTER 5

Callie

I sat on the couch in my living room with my laptop, researching images for a client commissioned work. They wanted a painting of a Blue Morpho butterfly, a rare species native to Latin America, so I was looking up reference photos to prepare a pencil drawing to paint later. As I flipped through the images, my mind wandered to my date with Ace the other night.

I still couldn't believe I'd opened up to him about the trust and the condition for me to inherit it. He'd just looked so damned sad when I shut down; I couldn't help it. There went my plan of keeping him at arm's length. I sighed, blowing a stray lock of hair out of my face as I continued to look through the butterfly images.

We'd ended the night on a positive note, but no mention of another date or being in touch. Just a few laughs, a quick hug goodbye, and a kiss on the cheek in the lobby before we went our separate ways. I wasn't sure how I felt about that, to be honest.

I knew more dates with Ace would only lead to heartache and disappointment for me, but I couldn't help but want them all the same. Something about him was magnetic, drawing me in, even though I could see the neon flashing "danger" signs all around him.

I thought about what he said about his situation with his dad. It seemed like he wanted to straighten his life out, only on his own terms, not his dad's. So that was a good sign; he knew he needed to make some changes. It seemed like he was under some pressure to do it fast, though. I wondered why.

I found a few butterfly photos that would work, so I printed them out in color on photo paper and taped them up on the wall next to my desk. I needed to do a pencil drawing first, but I was having trouble concentrating. I chewed on the end of my mechanical pencil, studying the photos and trying to decide where to start when my phone rang.

I didn't recognize the number, but since I was relieved to have a bit of a reprieve from starting my drawing, I answered it anyway.

"Hello?"

"You forgot to give me your number the other night."

I dropped the pencil, my drawing forgotten. It was Ace.

I quickly composed myself and answered, "Seems like you didn't have any trouble getting it, anyway."

He laughed. A deep, throaty sound that made my insides quiver. I shook that feeling off as he responded. "I had to sweet talk Cindy at Save the Children. It wasn't easy."

"Right. I'm sure the moment she heard your voice she offered to send you a complete dossier on me."

"Not quite, but I did get your number. So, what's up?"

I rolled my eyes, unable to suppress the smile that tugged at the corners of my mouth. That he'd called Cindy at the charity and talked her into giving him my number was sort of creepy but also sort of sweet at the same time. I had to admit; I was glad he did it.

"Just working on a client painting. You?"

"Just wondering where you're taking me for our second date."

A huge grin spread over my face. I couldn't help it. "Is that right?"

"Yeah, I mean, your grandmother spent a lot of money on these dates. We should give her what she paid for, right?"

I decided to play along against my better judgment. Why did he have to be so goddamn charming? "It would be rude not to."

"I'm glad we're on the same page, Ms. Harrison. How about Friday night? I'll pick you up, and you can surprise me. I love surprises." He laughed again, and I swore my heart skipped a beat.

"Sounds good, Mr. Dalton. I'll text you my address." I bit my lip, trying not to grin like a giddy teenager. Going out with him again was more than a bad idea; it was a terrible idea. But I thought about my talk with Grand-Mère the other day, about how I couldn't let my experience with Vic keep me from trying to find love again. Maybe this thing with Ace wouldn't lead to anything, but it felt like the time was right to try again, to open myself up to the possibility of finding love.

"No need, I have it already."

This time I laughed. "Thanks, Cindy."

It was settled. Ace and I were going on a second date.

Ace

"WHAT'S WITH YOU, MAN? YOU'RE JUST SO... HAPPY. IT'S weird, cut it out," Greg said, between bites of his turkey sandwich. We were having lunch in his office, listening to some music and talking sports, as usual. I stopped before taking a bite of my own sandwich to reply.

"What're you talking about?" But I knew. I couldn't help it. Knowing I was going to see Callie again soon had put me on cloud nine. Nothing could bring me down. Greg could tell me it was my day to clean the toilets, and I'd probably do it while whistling a little tune.

As soon as she'd left the restaurant that night, I'd realized I didn't have her number or any way to contact her. Calling Cindy at Save the Children had been my only hope, and luckily, I'm pretty persuasive. It didn't take much; a few compliments on how well the bachelor auction went, implying that Cindy herself had a lot to do with it. How I'd be so grateful if she could help me out and that I'd love to let her boss know what a stellar job she's doing for the Foundation. Boom. I had Callie's phone number and address, just like that. Too easy, actually.

Greg smirked while pushing his glasses up. "Well, you've had a gigantic smile plastered on your face all morning. Even when I told you your dad wanted to see you after lunch, it didn't phase you. What gives?"

The grin on my face got even wider. "I'm seeing Callie again."

Greg raised an eyebrow. "Really? She must be pretty desperate." He smiled, taking a big bite out of his sandwich.

"Yeah, desperate to see me again," I said with a laugh while flipping him the bird. I finished my sandwich, wadded up the wrapper, and shot it at the trashcan like a miniature basketball. I missed.

"At least your luck with women is better than your aim." Greg shot his own balled-up wrapper at the trashcan, making it in. He gloated while I rolled my eyes.

My phone chirped with an incoming text message. It was from Nick.

Get your ass in dad's office. Now.

I scowled, prompting Greg to shoot me a questioning look.

"I'm being summoned to the principal's office. I'll be back later. Hopefully." I shoved the phone in my pocket, feeling my good mood from earlier slipping away. So much for nothing being able to bring me down.

WHEN I ARRIVED, THE GOOD SONS WERE ALREADY seated in front of Dad's desk. There was paperwork scattered everywhere, a couple of laptops open, showing various photos of the fungus in question, and Dad sitting behind his desk, the vein in his forehead throbbing as he scowled when I entered the room.

"Horace, didn't Gregory give you my message? I said I wanted to see you after lunch," he growled while I took a seat between the golden boys.

I sighed. "Yeah, he did. I just finished lunch, and here I am. What's going on?"

Nick looked from me to Dad, then back at me. "We need your help."

I blinked several times. "Wait, what? Is this the Twilight Zone?"

Jasper gave me a disdainful look, shaking his head "no" slightly. Nick scoffed while Dad went red in the face.

"Cut the bullshit, Horace. I asked you in here because there's something you can do to help, and it's high time you did something, anyway."

My hackles raised instantly. "Wait a damn minute. I asked what I could do to help the other day, and you told me to just keep doing whatever Greg needed me to do. And that's what I did." My face flushed with anger. How dare he accuse me of not doing anything to help when he's the one who turned down my help when I offered.

He waved a hand in dismissal. "That was before. I have new information now."

"Okay. So, what can I do?" I asked with irritation.

Nick piped up this time. "Do you know a woman named Becky? You were seen with her at Indigo awhile back."

Becky. Becky. Indigo. I searched my brain. Oh. "Uh, yeah, I thought her name was Michelle. Why? And how do you even know about her?" *What the fuck? Do they have a private investigator on my ass now?*

Dad smacked his cane on the desk, the vein in his head threatening to pop any second. "Boy, this is serious business. We haven't processed one drop of liquor in over a week. We're starting to lay people off from their jobs, inventory is dwindling, and we can't commit to fulfilling new orders because of this goddamned lawsuit. Don't you think I have everyone I know on this, looking for something, anything, to get us out of this mess? Don't you think I'm using every resource available to me? Working every angle, leaving no stone unturned?"

I flinched when he struck the desk, growing more irritated as he spoke. He wanted to treat me like a child and then accuse me of being a child when I didn't understand what was going on. So damned frustrating, but I bit my tongue. If Dad could work every angle, so could I. If he needed my help so fucking badly, there'd better be something in it for me.

"I get it. What do you need me for, Dad?" I asked through gritted teeth.

"Becky works for the law firm of Emery & Knight. They're working for the Environmental Council that instigated this whole class-action lawsuit," Jasper quietly supplied while Dad and I glared at one another.

Nick laughed. "Looks like your man-whoring might finally pay off, Ace."

"SHUT UP!" Dad bellowed, letting his hard gaze roam over all three of us. Silence filled the room as we stared at him. After a few moments, he spoke, his voice low, calm, and icy.

"Horace, you will see Becky again. Find out whatever you can get out of her about this lawsuit. What angles they're pursuing, people involved, anything she'll tell you. Bring the information back to us, and we'll see if we can use any of it." He said it as if there was no debate. I had news for him, though.

"Excuse the fuck out of me, but I don't think so." I stood, preparing to march out of his office, out of this building, and straight to the bar. Jasper sighed, and Nick chuckled, both looking to Dad for a reaction.

"Oh, 'you don't think so.' Let me tell you some —" Dad started, but I cut him off mid-sentence.

"No, let ME tell YOU something. Only a few weeks ago, you told me to get my shit together, took my credit cards, and made me start working here. And I'm trying. Fuck, I'm trying, Dad," I said, running one hand through my curls. I turned to face him with a shrug. "But now that it's convenient for you, now that it might help you out, you want me to go back to doing exactly what you condemned me for? It's bullshit."

I shook my head, glaring at the three of them, anger swelling inside me. They were essentially asking me to fuck Becky again to get information out of her. Fucking hypocrites, every one of them.

I thought about Callie. The only good thing to happen to me in who knew how long. How she'd resisted opening up to me at the restaurant. When she finally did, it felt amazing that she had trusted me enough to let me in. I couldn't do something like this and risk fucking up a good thing before it even started.

"No," I said firmly. Before any of them could say another word, I turned and stormed out, slamming the door behind me.

I KEPT A LOW PROFILE AT WORK FOR THE NEXT COUPLE OF days. Things were strained enough as it was. Not only was Dad in rare form, but Nick, Jasper, and almost everyone else at Dalton Enterprises seemed to be on edge because of this damned lawsuit. Even Greg, normally so easygoing, was irritable and much busier than usual. So, I stayed in one corner of his office, doing the busy work he gave me to do, and working on my poem when I had a few minutes free.

Around lunchtime, I decided to walk down the street to a new pizza joint to grab lunch for Greg and me. He was on the phone and barely acknowledged me when I mouthed to him I was leaving, so I headed out, making sure to take the long way so I could avoid walking past Dad's office.

When I reached the lobby, I stopped in my tracks. I couldn't believe what I was seeing.

What the fuck.

Becky, my one-night stand from Indigo, was at the

reception desk. She turned just then and saw me, her face lighting up as she started towards me. *Oh, fuck no.*

"Ace! There you are!" she called as she crossed the lobby. Her long blonde hair was pulled up into a high pony-tail, and she wore a black, skin-tight mini-skirt, a red halter top that crisscrossed at the neck, and red stilettos. Her bright red lips stretched into a wide grin as she approached while I stood there shitting myself.

"What are you doing here?" I asked, the first words to come to mind falling out of my mouth.

She laughed, a soft tinkling little sound. "You invited me for lunch, silly."

I did what?

I was about to tell her I did no such thing when I felt someone grab my arm. I turned to find my brother, Nick, a cocky grin on his face.

"Excuse me, may I borrow my brother for just one minute?"

Oh fuck. This was a setup. Since I wouldn't do it will-ingly, they'd taken matters into their own hands. I clenched my jaw, my face heating as I looked at him.

"Oh, sure! I'll just be right over here, Ace," she said brightly, then moved to the waiting area to sit on a couch underneath a large White Wolf logo.

When she was out of earshot, I turned on my brother. "What the fuck, man?"

He held his hands up. "Look, it was Dad's idea. He really wants an inside scoop from that law firm, and your relationship with her is the only thing we have."

"There is NO relationship. It was one night. This is bullshit, and you know it." I scrubbed one hand over my face and sighed.

"Hey, I don't call the shots around here. Not yet, anyway. Just get some info to satisfy Dad, okay?" He

73

slapped my back a little too hard and walked away, leaving me to face Becky on my own.

I looked over to where she sat. She grinned and waved. What the fuck was I gonna do now? I turned away from her, rubbing the stubble on my jaw while I thought. Alright, I could do this without fucking her. I charmed Cindy at the Foundation into giving me Callie's number over the phone. I could do this.

Callie.

Just thinking of her while Becky sat waiting for me in the lobby made my heart sink. I had to make this quick, get some info for Dad, and get Becky out of my life. And since he was forcing my hand, I would have a talk with dear old Dad after lunch and make sure he knew the terms of this deal. Twenty thousand dollars, to be exact.

CHAPTER 6

Callie

I walked into the small coffee shop in Green Hills, looking around for my friend, Sarah. I saw her sitting at a table for two in the corner, where she waved to me. The scent of freshly brewed coffee filled the air while people sat at tables and in armchairs, most of them with some sort of electronic device in front of them. I weaved through them all to reach Sarah, who smiled broadly as I approached.

"Babe!" she greeted me. She stood, pulling me into a quick hug before we sat down. A cup of my favorite coffee already sat in front of me, thanks to her.

"Hey girl, how's married life treating you?" I asked. I took a sip of my coffee, savoring the richness and the sweet notes of the caramel flavoring. Sarah and her new husband had rushed off to Vegas after the bachelorette party to get married. That's what they wanted, just the two of them, an

Elvis impersonator, and a couple of random strangers as witnesses. They'd just returned from their wedding slash honeymoon, and Sarah had wasted no time in setting up a coffee date to catch up.

She grinned slyly at me, raising an eyebrow. "It's fantastic. But we'll come back to that later. What's this the girls are saying about you going out with Nashville's most infamous playboy, Ace Dalton? I want deets."

I tried to suppress a smile while rolling my eyes in mock exasperation. I figured it would be the first thing on today's agenda; I knew my friend too well.

"Oh, come on. I need to hear about Vegas first!" I laughed, trying to stall. I wasn't sure what to say about the Ace situation, to be honest.

She groaned. "Later! Spill it!" She blew on her coffee before taking a sip, staring at me expectantly.

Here goes nothing.

"Well… long story short, Grand-Mère won some dates with him for me at a bachelor auction."

Her mouth dropped open. "No!"

I laughed, nodding. "Yep. I had no idea until it was too late. I didn't want to do it at first…" I trailed off, and she cocked her head to the side quizzically.

"Go on," she said, dragging out the second word while she gestured with one hand for me to continue.

I sighed. "You know what happened with Vic. And Ace has a reputation." I shrugged.

Sarah raised an eyebrow at me, smiling. "Honey, Ace Dalton is a lot of things, but Vic ain't one of 'em."

I scowled at her. "How do you know so much about him, anyway?"

"In college, my roommate 'went out' with him a few times," she said, exaggerating the "went out" and using air quotes. "I heard a lot of stories about him, girl. He may have screwed nearly every woman in Davidson county, but he's actually a nice guy." She shrugged, taking a sip of her coffee before continuing. "Vic, however, was NOT a nice guy. You're talking night and day here, babe."

I thought about that for a moment while I blew on my coffee before taking another sip. Maybe Sarah was right. Ace did seem like a genuinely nice guy; I honestly couldn't see him treating me the way Vic did. Maybe I had been thinking about this all wrong.

"So, how did the first date go?" she asked, grinning from ear to ear, her blue eyes sparkling.

I pursed my lips against a smile that threatened to emerge on my face. "It wasn't bad, actually. It started out a little rough because I had my guard up, but we ended up talking, and it was... nice." I scrunched up my nose and shrugged.

"That's a good start, 'nice.' And when is the next date?"

I took a deep breath. "This Saturday, actually. I'm supposed to plan it, and I'm drawing a blank. Help?" I asked, giving her puppy dog eyes.

She put one finger to her lips, thinking. "How about... a picnic? You could go to Centennial Park. Have a cute little picnic and see what develops afterward?" She smiled devilishly and raised one eyebrow at me.

I laughed. "I don't know... maybe?" I asked, thinking about it. It sounded good, but what would he think? Too cute?

She shrugged. "I think it's perfect. And I can guarantee you no other girl he's been with has taken him on a picnic date."

I grinned. "Oh, you can guarantee that, can you?"

"Yep. I'd bet my left tit on it."

I nearly spit my coffee out at that. "Okay, challenge

accepted. For your left tit's sake, I hope you're right. Now, tell me about Vegas!"

I half-heartedly listened to her talk about the Elvis impersonator who married them, the hotel, the shows they saw, the food they ate. All the while thinking about Ace and wondering how our next date would go.

Ace

I CHECKED MY REFLECTION IN THE REARVIEW MIRROR OF my Jeep before heading to Callie's front door. I felt on edge, but it had nothing to do with Callie or our date. It was Becky. Fucking Becky.

Dad's little setup the other day had been a nightmare. Becky had been under the impression that I had asked her out to lunch; I'd even tried to tell her it was a misunderstanding, but she wasn't hearing any of it. I had ended up taking her to a pizza place a couple of blocks away from the office, paranoid about being seen with her the entire time. And after all of that, I still didn't get any relevant information out of her about the case.

This was only my second date with Callie, but I could tell this was different. I actually *liked* her. I couldn't remember the last time I liked a woman and didn't just want to get into her pants. I mean, I wanted to get into her pants, too. I wasn't a monk. Callie had a smoking hot body, and I wanted to explore every inch of it. But she was intelligent, creative, and independent, too. She didn't look at me the way everyone else did—as a failure, a screw-up, or just a good fuck. She talked to me like she saw something in me that I couldn't even see in myself, and it made me want to be that person.

What the fuck was happening to me? Getting all sappy and shit. I just didn't want to fuck this up before it even got started, not when I already liked her so damn much. Fucking Becky. No way would Dad accept that I wasn't able to get any information out of her; he'd demand that I produce something that would help the case if I expected him to pay my debt with Andre. And I had a feeling Becky wouldn't be opposed to seeing me again, either.

I ran a hand through my blond curls and sighed. I looked down at myself before I knocked—my Kiton khaki pants, perfectly creased, and Berluti leather loafers, paired with a white Brunello Cucinelli button-down shirt, with the sleeves rolled up to my elbows to show off my ink. I wore my silver Breitling watch and a few silver rings on my fingers as well. I may not have any money right now, but at least I still had my expensive wardrobe. I took a deep breath and knocked on her door.

After a moment, Callie answered. She beamed at me, her dark brown hair with subtle golden highlights hanging in loose waves around her shoulders. She wore a purple sundress with leather sandals, and her deep blue eyes sparkled as she held the door open for me. *Fucking beautiful.*

"Hey, you," she said as I slipped past her into the house. It was small but cozy, with a living room and kitchen-dinette all mashed into one space. There was a sectional couch, a television, and a kitchen area with a small dining table and chairs. I noticed a canvas on an easel near the couch, a palette, brushes, and a paint-splattered apron nearby.

It was a gorgeous painting of a field of sunflowers, the sun setting behind them in tones of pink, orange, and purple. It looked so real. I was speechless for a few seconds before turning to her while gesturing towards the canvas.

"You painted that?" I asked, feeling ridiculous after the words came out.

She smiled softly, turning her attention to the canvas. "Yeah, I did. Or, I am. It's not finished."

I turned back to the painting. "Looks pretty damn good to me."

She laughed. "You like sunflowers?"

I faced her again and all the worries I'd had outside in the Jeep about Dad, Becky, and Andre... gone. Her smile made it all fade away. "Never really thought about it before, but yeah, I guess I like sunflowers. I'm assuming you're a big fan of them?"

"They're my favorite flower." She walked over to me, so we stood side by side, staring at her painting.

My gaze moved to her while she studied her own work. I cocked my head, admiring her. She was taller than most of the women I'd been with before, only a few inches shorter than my six-foot-three frame. I watched as she studied her painting, her brow drawn and her lips forming a sexy pout. "Why are they your favorite?"

"The Greek myth about Apollo and Clytie." She glanced at me and saw no recognition of this myth on my face, then continued. "Clytie was a sea nymph. She loved Apollo, the Sun God, and he loved her back until he fell for someone else. Clytie was incredibly jealous. She ruined Apollo's new relationship, and in his anger, his heart hardened towards her. She never stopped loving him, and she spent her days watching him as he moved the sun across the sky in his chariot. Eventually, she transformed into a sunflower, which turns its head to always face the sun," she said, not taking her eyes from the painting, lost in thought. "She never stopped loving him."

We stood there quietly for a few moments before she spoke. "Sorry, you probably don't care about Greek myths," she said, jarring herself from her reverie. She cut her eyes at me and smiled shyly.

I shoved my hands into my pockets and grinned back. "It's a cool story. I'd never heard of it before."

She tucked a strand of hair behind her ear and glanced away from me, her face flushed. Something about that made a wave of warmth flood my body. I had an overwhelming urge to pull her to me, kiss her pouty lips deeply while letting my hands explore her body. My cock twitched in agreement with that plan, but I shoved those thoughts aside.

"We should probably go. Let me get a few things, and we'll head out, okay?"

I cleared my throat and shook my head, trying to rid myself of that fantasy. "Sounds good."

She nodded, then turned towards the kitchen area while I quickly pulled my cell phone out of my pocket and snapped a photo of her sunflower painting. I wasn't even sure why I wanted a picture of it. I just knew I did. Maybe to keep a little part of her with me after our date was over? *Look at me, being a big ol' sap.*

Callie came back just as I was putting my phone away, laden with a picnic basket and a tote bag. The corners of my mouth tugged upward in a grin.

"Are you taking me on a picnic?"

"I am, if that's okay with you? Centennial Park, maybe near The Parthenon? We can walk around the park afterward. Maybe there will be some live music or something else going on." She bit her lip, one eyebrow raised, waiting for me to approve.

I walked to her and took the picnic basket out of her hand, letting my fingers gently graze down her arm as I did.

81

"I can't think of a better way to spend the afternoon. Lead the way."

She blushed, beaming at me, and I followed her out the door of her house and down the driveway to her Mustang, admiring how her ass looked in that dress as we walked. When I felt my cock hardening while I watched her, for a moment, I wished we could just stay in for some Netflix and chill time. But I knew I wanted to handle this differently than all the other chicks I'd been with. I didn't just want to fuck Callie; I wanted to get to know her. And I wanted her to get to know me, too. That meant taking it slow and not putting the moves on her right away. I sighed as I put the picnic basket in the backseat, and as I did, my phone chirped with a text message. I absently pulled my phone out to see who it was from as I got into her car on the passenger side.

Lunch was so much fun, babe! Let's do it again soon, maybe Tuesday? Lmk

The message was followed by several heart emojis. I cringed. Fucking Becky.

Callie

"WELL, WHAT DO YOU THINK?" I ASKED, GESTURING TO A spot on the lawn in front of The Parthenon in Centennial Park. It was a beautiful, sunny day without a single cloud in the sky. The area we were in was off the beaten path, near a little flower bed, but still within view of all the action so we could people watch. They were everywhere—walking dogs, jogging, playing with children, and taking photos. There was activity all around, but this spot still seemed like its own secluded little bubble to me.

Ace had looked a little distracted ever since we left the house. Even now, he was looking around, his handsome face drawn into a scowl as if searching for someone else. He wasn't paying attention to a word I said.

"What? Oh, yeah, this is great."

I frowned but didn't say anything. I took the blanket out of my tote bag and laid it down on the ground while he started unloading the picnic basket. His brow furrowed, his pouty mouth turned down in a frown. I couldn't ignore it any longer.

"Something wrong, Ace?"

He stopped what he was doing and sighed. "Sorry. It's just a work issue. I'll try to stop thinking about it."

I nodded while we started making our sandwiches, studying him. He was scorching hot in his khakis and white button-down shirt, tattoos on display with the sleeves rolled up. I resisted the urge to reach out a finger to trace the black lines of ink on his forearm. Everything about him was perfect, except the frown on his gorgeous face. "Would it help to talk about it?"

He grimaced. "No, no. It's fine. This chicken salad is awesome. Did you make it?"

"I did, thanks."

We ate in silence for a few minutes, then his phone trilled an alert for a text message. He ignored it, to his credit, until it went off again a few minutes later. He looked at me apologetically as he reached for his phone to take a look.

I saw his jaw clench as he read, his mouth pursed into a straight line.

I stuck a potato chip into my mouth as he put the phone away and went back to his lunch as if nothing had happened. Some kids ran by, chasing a dog while laughing. I smiled, then noticed Ace glaring after them.

"You know, if you're not having fun, we don't have to do this." I put my sandwich down on the paper plate next to me and leveled my gaze at him. His eyes were dark and stormy, his jaw clenched. I hated seeing him so stressed out and wished I had the nerve to move closer and wrap my arms around him. But if he didn't want to be here with me, I didn't want to force him.

His face softened as he shook his head. "I am having fun, Callie. I'm sorry, it's just... there's so much bullshit happening at work. In my life, in general. I can't seem to get away from it." He looked down, brushing a few blades of grass from his pants.

"What kind of bullshit? Sometimes just talking about it helps." I cocked my head at him and risked reaching out to touch his hand lying next to me on the blanket. The feel of his skin on mine was almost electric, sending a thrill through me and making the butterflies in my stomach take flight.

He sighed, flipping his hand over to give mine a squeeze, then looked off into the distance where a photographer was taking portraits of a woman in a wedding gown. "You already know about my dad and his ultimatum. Now the company is being sued by some environmental agency, something about the alcohol that evaporates during the whiskey's aging process being a catalyst for this fungus to grow. It's covering buildings and other structures all over the area, and they're blaming Dalton Enterprises for it. They've filed a cease and desist order, so there's no whiskey production right now. Dad is livid."

He pulled a weed nearby and tossed it while he spoke before looking at me, still holding my hand in his. I felt like he was holding something back. But this was a good start, at least.

"Wow. I'm sure your dad has all the best people working on it, right?" I asked, acutely aware of my hand in his, trying to calm the butterflies still swirling around inside me.

He sighed, turning to look at me. "Yeah, I guess."

"It's nice that you're worried about it, though. Seems to me like something someone who is 'getting their shit together' would do," I said with a small smile, nudging his shoulder with mine.

He huffed a laugh. "Yeah, I'm trying." He gave me a dejected look, then shook his head, finally releasing my hand.

"That's all anyone can ask you to do," I said with a shrug, surprised I was already mourning the loss of his touch.

"You don't know my dad."

I bit the inside of my lip. I didn't know what else to say. I didn't know his dad or his relationship with Ace, but I got the feeling it was strained and went way back. For now, I'd just be happy he put a crack in the wall, letting a little bit of light through. I felt cautiously optimistic, which I'd rate as an improvement on how I'd felt about him before today. Ace definitely wasn't Vic, but he came with his own unique set of baggage, just the same.

"Hey, why don't we see what else is going on in the park? Maybe we can find some live music to listen to?" I asked, deciding to get his mind off of his problems.

He met my gaze, the corners of his mouth slowly turning up in a smile. I saw his brow soften, his entire demeanor loosening up before my eyes. My heart squeezed as those bright blue eyes twinkled just for me.

I should've been panicking; I should've been running in

the opposite direction. My head kept reminding me this could only end badly for me, but my heart screamed at me to throw caution to the wind and go for it. As I worked through my inner dilemma, his gaze traveled over my face, down my chest and hips, lighting my body on fire as it did.

"Yeah, okay. Let's do it," Ace said with a slight grin. He stood up and reached a hand out to pull me to my feet as well. I overcompensated when I stood, which sent me crashing into his chest. With a giggle, I looked up at him.

"Sorry," I said, meeting his eyes, which had softened even more. An easy smile erupted on his face as he wrapped his arms around me, intentionally pulling me closer. I hadn't expected that, but I let him. My hands rested on his chest, but I found them weaving their way up around his neck. Our gazes were firmly locked on one another, and as the laughter subsided, I felt something else taking its place. Something that made my blood feel as if it were on fire.

I leaned into him and felt his lips on mine, softly at first, then gaining in urgency. I kissed him back with just as much fervor, my pulse racing as this sudden desire for Ace left me with an ache in my core. I parted my lips to him, letting his tongue find mine, fueling the fire of my yearning for him.

His hands trailed down the back of my dress and over my ass, the flimsy material a thin barrier between his skin and mine. A little moan escaped my lips as his fingers dug into my flesh, pressing me against the evidence of his desire for me, making me forget where we were. It felt as if we were the only two people on the planet, and time had stood still for us.

At the shrill sound of a catcall, Ace broke the kiss, releasing my ass and backing away. He shot me a cocky half-grin before looking around for the offending whistler, his hand grazing down my arm and catching my hand. My heart still hammered in my chest as I fought to catch my breath. A small smile played on my lips as I watched Ace, thinking about how we must have looked, standing here, making out in the middle of the park. My other hand rose unbidden to touch my lips, which still tingled from our kiss.

"How about that walk you promised me?" he asked with a wink, still holding my hand. There was no denying the physical attraction between us, but there was something else there, too. His thumb stroked the back of my hand for a few seconds as he smiled at me, almost as if he couldn't believe it either.

I liked him. I actually liked Ace Dalton.

CHAPTER 7

Ace

idnight blue? Cobalt? I deleted the line I had just written and scrubbed one hand over my face, putting my phone down. All I could think about was Callie and her deep blue eyes. And then I thought about how she looked at me at the end of our picnic date, and my heart shattered. No one had ever looked at me like she did, like I was worth something. Like I mattered. Like she believed in me.

Fuck. I ran a hand through my disheveled curls, guilt blooming in my chest. She doesn't know the real me yet, the fuck up, but she's about to find out. And it was going to destroy me to see the look in her eyes when she did.

I leaned back into the plush leather couch in the large sitting room of my parents' house. My phone dinged with another text; I'd been getting them all morning. Andre, reminding me how much time I had left to get his $20k.

Greg, asking me if I was watching the game. A local sports bookie letting me know I'd won $500 on a bet I placed last week. *Great, that'll go a long way on what I owed Andre.* I picked up my phone, cringing when I saw who it was from.

Babe, want to meet for drinks later? I miss you. Followed by a bunch of kissy face emojis.

Fucking Becky. I took a deep breath as I tried to figure out what to reply when Dad tottered into the study, leaning heavily on his cane. I put the phone down again, preparing myself. I was sure I wasn't going to like it, whatever it was.

"There you are, son. I've been looking all over for ya," he said with his deep Southern drawl, in a tone much milder than I expected. He worked his way slowly to the leather chair by the fireplace across from me, where he finally sat down heavily and propped his cane up on the armrest.

"What's up, Dad?" I asked. Since he wasn't going for the jugular just yet, I decided I'd play nice as well.

He took a few shallow breaths as if the effort of walking into the room had done him in. He gripped the armrests of the chair, his jowls sagging and his bushy eyebrows drooping. It occurred to me that this lawsuit was probably taking a lot out of the old bastard. He wasn't a spring chicken anymore and probably had more health problems than any of us knew about; the additional stress of the class action lawsuit wasn't doing him any favors.

"Are you having any luck getting any information out of the girl?"

There it was. I leaned forward, propping my elbows on my knees, clasping my hands, and resting my chin on them. I gave him a long look before huffing a laugh.

"How's it feel, Dad? For once, I can finally do something the golden boys can't do. You need me. Must be eating you up inside."

His face fell in defeat, which shocked me and made me feel a little guilty for what I'd just said. Even though he deserved it.

"Horace, I'm sorry I've made you feel less than for all these years. I couldn't see it before, but I'm seeing it now." His blue eyes glimmered as if tears threatened to fall.

I had no idea what to do with this. Who was this man, and what did he do with my father, the hardass? The all-mighty CEO of Dalton Enterprises, who took no shit from anyone? I had to admit, he appealed to my emotions with this "act" or whatever it was, the boy deep inside of me who always longed for his father's approval. But the man I'd become said it was too little, too late.

I laughed bitterly, looking him square in the eyes. "Yeah, well, you made me the man I am today. So, thanks for that."

That seemed to bust whatever emotional bubble he'd been in. His bushy brows drew together, and his sagging mouth formed a deep frown. He waved his hand in the air dismissively. "That's neither here nor there, boy. Tell me what you've found out, anything?"

I clenched my jaw. It was now or never.

"Dad, I don't like this game you're playing with me. Using me as a pawn whenever it suits your end game, then condemning me for the same actions when it doesn't. I'm gonna get the information from Becky, but not for you. I'm doing it for Nick and Jasper so that this company and their futures don't go to shit. I know you're doing it for them too, so let's just agree on that and make a deal, shall we?"

He sputtered, his frown deepening. "A deal? What the hell are you talking about?"

"Just what I said. You need me. And I need one last thing from you before you can consider me out of your hair and on the straight and narrow." I met his incredulous gaze. I could see the wheels turning in his head.

"And what might that be?"

"I'll get you the information. I'll get you all the information Becky has, and you can do whatever you please with it. I need $20k. Today."

Shit. I'd done it. My insides were quaking while I tried to hold it together on the outside. I didn't have much time left. I needed to get the money to Andre, and fast. I suppressed the urge to vomit and held his hard, stony gaze.

He leaned back, studying me silently for a few moments. A faint smile cracked his icy facade. With a slight shake of his head, he muttered, "You're just like me, you know. Always driving a hard bargain, always making sure there's something in it for you."

I felt my face heat with anger, my blood boiling. Before I could open my mouth for a retort, he continued.

"Fine. But I need something I can use first. Get me that, and you'll have your money, Horace."

Callie

I ARRIVED AT GRAND-MÈRE'S HOUSE BEARING A CHICKEN casserole I'd made earlier that morning. Since I'd bailed on our weekly Saturday afternoon tea yesterday so I could go out with Ace again, I thought I'd make it up to her by delivering Sunday brunch. The casserole was actually from one of her own recipes; it was always my favorite meal when I was growing up. The aroma coming from the warm dish I now held in my arms made my mouth water as I waited for her to open the front door.

She answered the door with a wide smile and beckoned me inside. "Ma chère, I wasn't expecting you today!" I slid past her into the pristine living room, where not a throw pillow was out of place. She shooed me forward into the attached kitchen, where I sat the casserole dish down on the counter.

"I know, Grand-Mère. But I wanted to see you since I had to cancel our tea yesterday." I turned to face her after removing the foil from the dish to find her smiling smugly at me, her arms crossed. She wore a navy blue twinset with cream-colored linen pants, her dark brown hair pulled up into a bun, which accentuated the gray streaks in it. As usual, I marveled that she didn't look like a woman in her seventies at all. Instead, she could've easily passed for her late-fifties.

"So, how was your date? And that casserole smells *magnifique*," she added in her soft French accent, her dark blue eyes sparkling mischievously as she watched me squirm. I suppressed a smile while biting the inside of my lip. I wanted to share how well the date had gone, how much I liked Ace, but I also didn't want her to get her hopes up about the trust. I didn't need her to start wedding planning when this thing with Ace was so new; it could end just as quickly as it began at this point.

I shrugged, turning back to the cabinets. I pulled out a couple of plates and searched in a drawer for a knife and a serving spoon for the casserole as I chose my words carefully. "Oh, I don't know, I wouldn't really call it a 'date.' It was fun though, I guess." I finished making a plate for Grand-Mère and turned to find her scowling at me as I handed it to her.

"Come now, *bébé*. I know better. I can tell; you haven't stopped glowing since you arrived. Tell me," she said, taking a chair at the small dinette table attached to her kitchen.

Well, so much for playing it cool. I took my plate and joined her at the table, taking a moment to savor a mouthful of the delicious casserole before I started talking. I wanted to make sure I didn't make it sound too good. The date had gone well, or so I believed, but I needed to downplay it for her sake.

"We went to Centennial Park for a picnic. See, that's so silly. It wasn't even a proper date," I said between bites. I watched as she tried the casserole, carefully tasting as she cocked her head, then finally nodding in approval as she took another bite.

When she heard the word "picnic," she nearly dropped her fork. "A picnic! That's wonderful! In fact, that's the best date of all, *très romantique*. Tell me more." She rose from her chair, going to the refrigerator to retrieve a pitcher of lemonade and two glasses from the cabinet while I stalled.

"Romantic? I wouldn't call it that. I mean, we just ate some chicken salad sandwiches and then walked around the park. There was a guy singing and playing his guitar, so we listened for a while, and that was it," I explained with a shrug, leaving out the juiciest details while she passed me a glass. My mouth had grown dry as I spoke, so I welcomed the tart lemonade and the few moments of reprieve it allowed me to think.

She cut her eyes at me, obviously thinking otherwise but deciding not to argue with me. "It sounds like the two of you had a wonderful time. When will you see him again?"

I shook my head as I finished chewing my last bite. "I don't know, Grand-Mère. We didn't talk about it. He only owes me one more date anyway, so please, don't get your hopes up about this." I decided to address it head-on with her. Aside from my own heart, I worried about her feelings getting hurt over this as well. I gave her a stern look I hoped conveyed how serious I was.

"Ma chère, don't worry about me. What is meant to be will be, no matter what I think. But... I think that you're falling for him, despite yourself." She gave me a knowing look with a quick wink before returning to her brunch.

I sputtered. "What? No. I'm not falling for Ace. That would be insane."

"Of course not. What was I thinking?" she asked, the corners of her mouth twitching as she glanced at me.

I shrugged. "I mean, you were right. He's definitely not like Vic. He has some issues, but who doesn't? He seems nice." I pushed the remnants of my food around on my plate as I spoke, avoiding her eyes.

"I understand," she said, a twinkle in her eyes and a grin playing on her thin lips. "Now, let's clean up these dishes and go sit in the garden for a while. You can tell me your plans for the third date."

Callie

I LAID MY WET PAINTBRUSHES ON A TOWEL BY THE SINK to dry while I put away my paint tubes for the day. It was late, and I'd spent hours working on the Blue Morpho butterfly painting for my client. I'd also spent the day distracted by thoughts of Ace and the episode in the park on Saturday. Now that it was over, my brain had sounded the alarm, telling me to back off, that nothing good could come of my attraction to him. But the memory of his hands on me, his tongue meeting mine with such urgency, how my heart raced while we made out in the middle of Centennial Park… it made me clench my thighs together even now and sent a warm sensation straight to my core. Just those few moments promised so much more… if I wanted it. And God help me, I wanted it.

I changed into a long t-shirt that doubled as a nightgown and shimmied out of my jeans upstairs in my bedroom. Moonlight streamed in through the large half-circle window above my bed, casting the entire room in a bluish glow. I climbed into bed, looking out the window at the stars, and found myself wondering what Ace was up to tonight.

My phone vibrated on the nightstand, alerting me to a text message. I was half asleep, so I closed my eyes again, figuring I'd answer it in the morning. A few seconds later, it vibrated again. I sighed in frustration. Who would text me so late? Even Sarah never texted me past ten. *Maybe it was Grand-Mère, and it was an emergency?* I rolled over, grabbing the phone off the table next to the bed.

Ace: r u still up?

Ace: this is crazy, but I can't stop thinking about u.

I bit my lip while a small smile crept over my face. The butterflies stirred in the pit of my stomach as I thought about my reply.

Me: We're both crazy then because I've thought about that kiss all day.

Three bubbles popped up to indicate he was texting back, which made me irrationally happy and anxious at the same time.

Ace: same. that little sound u made when I grabbed ur ass <devil emoji>

I felt my face flush as I grinned at the glowing screen in front of me.

Me: I don't know what you're talking about, sir.

Ace: keep calling me sir and i'll have to come over there right now. so what r u wearing? <wink emoji>

I paused, knowing where this was going. Ace was approaching it as a joke, casting out this cheesy line so I could opt out with dignity if I wanted to. I'd never sexted before. Did I want to take the bait, though? Hell yeah, I did.

Me: well, if you really want to know… I just got in bed so I'm just wearing a t-shirt and panties.

Ace: are u trying to kill me woman? <fire emoji x 3>

Me: hey you're the one who asked LOL

Ace: so tell me about these panties

Me: really? Lol

Ace: i never joke about panties <devil emoji>

Me: I had no idea you were so serious about women's lingerie. They're purple lace string bikini.

Ace: i may need a photo for verification purposes

Me: you'll just have to use your imagination for now. Maybe if you're lucky, you'll get to see them in person one day <wink emoji>

Ace: i have been feeling pretty lucky lately, actually

Me: so how about you? Let me guess, you sleep in the nude

Ace: <devil emoji x 3>

Me: <flame emoji x 3>

Ace: if i was there, you'd be sleeping nude too

Me: love the confidence <wink>

Ace: not confidence, just a fact

Me: so what else would be happening… if you were here?

I wouldn't usually be so bold, but somehow the memory of the park and knowing Ace couldn't stop thinking about it either filled me with confidence. As I laid in my bed with one of the hottest men I've ever seen on the other end of this conversation, I felt a warmth blooming in my core. I watched with bated breath as the three bubbles danced on the screen while he typed.

Ace: well, like I said, u'd be naked and i'd be exploring every inch of ur gorgeous body with my tongue. how does that sound for starters?

Me: it sounds good. really good <devil emoji>

Ace: and now i'm imagining that moan again <eggplant emoji>

Me: maybe I'm making that sound right now…

My phone vibrated in my hands with an incoming call from Ace. I smiled, biting my lip as I answered.

"Hi."

"You can't tell me that and expect me not to call. I wanna hear it," he said, his deep southern drawl practically whispering into the phone, sending a brand new spark of desire through my body. I took a deep breath.

"Tell me what you want me to do."

"First, get rid of those clothes."

I held the phone between my shoulder and my ear as I shimmied out of my panties, tossing them on the floor by the bed. Then I pulled the oversized t-shirt up and over my head quickly, barely breaking contact with the phone. I dropped it on the floor as well.

"Done," I breathed into the phone. I rarely slept naked when I was alone, which I had been for a long time now. The cool of the sheets against my flushed skin was a sensation I'd grown unaccustomed to, but it only heightened my senses as I felt myself growing damp between my legs.

"Good. I want you to touch yourself, pretend it's me doing it. I'm rubbing your clit in slow circles, applying just the right amount of pressure. How does that feel, Callie?" he asked, his voice low and deep.

I did as he asked, and it felt so good. I closed my eyes, imagining it was his fingers against me. My breath came a little faster as I worked my fingers over my clit. "Mmmm…"

He groaned, hearing me moan for him. "Yes, baby, like that. Now, insert a couple of fingers for me."

"Are you touching yourself, too?" I asked while doing what he asked me to do. I began to pump my fingers in and out of myself, feeling how slick I'd become.

"Mmmmhmmmm," he sighed into the phone.

God, just thinking about him, lying there naked in all his glory, getting turned on by the sounds I was making for him, almost sent me over the edge. I worked my fingers in and out, hitting just the right spot on my inner walls. I moaned again and heard what sounded like a growl on the other end of the line.

"Ace, I wish you were here," I breathed, the pressure building inside of me. With the phone lodged between my shoulder and my ear, I used my other hand to cup one breast. I teased my nipple between two fingers. "I'm so wet for you."

"Baby, one day I will be there, and I'll do everything you're doing to yourself now and more. I'll lick every square inch of that gorgeous body of yours until you come harder than you ever have before," he said, breathlessly, punctuated by a groan at the end of his sentence.

I couldn't believe I was so turned on, alone and naked in my bed. Picturing him masturbating on the other end of the line while thinking about what I was doing to myself for him spurred me on. I didn't hold back. I let out all the moans, sighs, and gasps, calling out his name as I fell apart. He followed close behind with a groan, my name a breathy sigh on his lips. If I could hear the sound of him coming every day of my life, I'd be the happiest woman on the planet.

"Fuck, Callie..." he sighed, sounding as if he were trying to put himself back together. My heart raced in my chest as I came back down from my high, a lazy smile on my face.

"Damn." It was all I could muster. My limbs lay sprawled to either side, my body spent and sweaty in the moonlight.

His ragged breaths continued over the phone while I pictured him in a similar state as me. I wished he were here so I could curl up against him, his warmth enveloping me as we drifted off into a blissful sleep together.

With that thought, I realized I'd taken yet another step into the danger zone tonight. I couldn't deny it any longer. I was falling for Ace. My poor heart be damned.

CHAPTER 8

Ace

"Fuck." I slammed my phone down on the bar, giving up on the poem I was working on. The words just weren't coming to me. I was too preoccupied with all the shit going on in my life right now. Yes, I'd gotten Dad to agree to pay my debt to Andre, but I had to get him some information from Becky first. And my time was running out. In fact, I was constantly looking over my shoulder, expecting to see the "Collection Agents" coming back at any moment. My nerves were shot between Andre, Dad, Becky, and my burgeoning relationship with Callie. I scrubbed my hands over my face before downing the last of my whiskey, wondering what the fuck I was going to do about it all.

"In the mood for a little company?"

I looked up to see my little brother, Jasper, sitting next to me at the bar. He gave me a sympathetic smile while waving to the bartender, who promptly took his order for a draft beer and nodded in acknowledgment to me when I pointed at my empty shot glass. I shook my head, a smirk on my face.

"Did Dad send you? Checking up on my progress, is he? Well, you can tell him to—"

"No, Dad didn't send me," Jas said, cutting me off. The bartender sat a tall mug of beer in front of him. He took a pull before continuing. "I wanted to see how you're holding up, and I knew you'd be here."

"How I'm 'holding up?'" I repeated. I rolled my eyes. Like any of them gave a damn. They just wanted me to do whatever it took to get the information they needed to get the whiskey production going again.

Jasper gave me a serious look. "Yeah, Ace. I don't agree with Dad, asking you to get information out of that poor girl. It's bullshit, and he knows it."

I raised my eyebrows, shocked to hear him challenging Dad's decision. I shrugged. "Thanks, Jas. But we both know, whatever Dad wants, Dad gets." I knocked back another shot of whiskey, loving the way it burned my throat on the way down. It wasn't White Wolf tonight. It seemed the bar was all out, but it was getting the job done just the same.

He cocked his head at me. "What does Ace want, though?" he asked, meeting my eyes.

I was silent for a moment, holding his gaze, then I huffed a laugh and looked away. "Nobody gives a damn what Ace wants, little brother." My head was feeling fuzzy from all the shots I'd had, and I wished he'd just leave me in peace to work on my shitty poem.

"You're wrong. What's going on with you, anyway? What happened with the dates from the bachelor auction? I disapproved of that also, but Dad overruled me, for what it's worth." He took a long drink of his beer while he waited for me to fill him in.

"The fucking bachelor auction. Yeah, her name is Callie. Her grandmother bought the dates for her. It's a long story. She's actually amazing, and I definitely don't deserve her," I said, my words slurring and coming out in a rush. I couldn't believe I was telling Jasper about Callie, but it was all true. I didn't deserve someone like her.

He winced and punched my arm. "Don't say shit like that, man. Of course you deserve to find a good girl and settle down. I hope she's the one, I really do."

I shook my head, a frown forming on my lips. "I'll fuck it up. Wait and see."

"Man, shut the fuck up. I've seen you the last few weeks. You've been trying to turn your shit around. You're gonna be okay, Ace," Jas said, downing the last of his beer.

"Not when she finds out about the money I owe Andre. And that I'm seeing Becky to get information out of her. I've been trying, Jas, but fuck. I just can't win." I slammed the shot glass on the bar, prompting the bartender to look at me with a frown.

"Andre? Who's that? How much do you owe him?" Jasper asked, narrowing his eyes at me.

"I placed a bet on a poker game. Dad canceled my cards, so I still owe Andre $20k," I said, the alcohol loosening my lips. Under normal circumstances, I wouldn't be telling Jasper about any of this shit.

"Twenty thousand? Damn, Ace." He ran a hand through his tousled blonde hair, blowing a low whistle as he did.

"Dad's gonna pay it. I've just... gotta talk to Becky first," I slurred. My cell phone trilled with an incoming text just then. I grabbed my phone and was startled to see Callie's name.

Hey you. Wanna come over tomorrow night? I'll cook and we can find something to binge on Netflix. Are you in?

I stared at her text for a few moments while Jasper kept asking me if something was wrong. "No, nothing's wrong," I told him. But everything was wrong.

I was about to fuck up the one good thing in my life right now. Once Callie found out I was seeing Becky, and she would, it would be all over with. It wouldn't matter why I was taking Becky out. Callie wouldn't want anything to do with me. And if she ever found out about my gambling debt? It would be the final nail in the coffin. It was true; I wasn't good enough for Callie, and I never would be. Everything I touched turned to shit, and I was about to prove that to her once and for all.

But I was a selfish son of a bitch. Her text made me long for her, made me think about how she moaned for me. I wanted to feel her silky, dark brown hair brush over my fingers. I wanted to feel her full, pouty lips on mine. I wanted to trace every line of her beautiful body with my tongue. I wanted to feel her hands on me, roaming over every inch of my skin. I wanted to know what it would feel like to be loved by her, even if it wasn't real. Even if I was about to fuck it up, I wanted to know what it was like so I could hold on to the memory of it long after she said goodbye to me. Because all I was ever going to have of Callie Harrison was a memory after I did what I had to do to save my own ass. And it felt like someone had plunged a dagger deep into my heart every time I imagined her midnight blue eyes brimming with tears because of me.

"Let me take you home, Ace," Jasper said softly, watching me as I read Callie's text.

"Yeah, okay, just a minute." I quickly typed out a response to her, careful not to misspell anything in my drunken state.

I'd love to. Just tell me what time and I'm there.

It would be our third date, the last one she was obligated to in order to fulfill her grandmother's auction purchase. It could be the last time I'd ever see her.

Callie

I CHECKED THE LASAGNA IN THE OVEN FOR THE SIXTH time since I'd put it in fifteen minutes ago. I knew it needed to cook for at least forty-five minutes, but I couldn't help myself. I paced around the kitchen, straightening up anything that looked out of place, then I made my way into the living room and did the same there as well. I fluffed cushions, folded throws and placed them over the back of the couch, and put a stack of DVDs, as well as the Firestick, on the coffee table for easy access. I stood back with my hands on my hips, admiring the orderly living room, and blew out a puff of air. I glanced at the clock. I had about twenty more minutes before Ace was supposed to arrive, so I headed up the stairs to the bedroom to finish getting myself ready.

I decided on a light yellow A-line dress that had tiny flowers printed on it. My long brown hair hung freely in loose waves over my shoulders. I figured I should keep it casual since we were staying in tonight. And I had to admit, staying in with Ace had my heart doing somersaults in my chest.

I looked myself over in the mirror, touching up my makeup and adding a pair of small gold hoop earrings, when I heard the doorbell ring. Startled, I looked at the clock on my bedroom wall to see he was right on time.

Tonight would either be the end of the road for us or the beginning of something brand new. I could feel it. Both possibilities left me breathless. I hurried down the stairs, the aroma of warm lasagna filling my lungs as I made my way to the front door. I took a deep breath and opened it. And there he was, six-feet-three inches of smoldering gorgeousness, standing right in front of me.

Ace stood on my doorstep, his blonde curls tousled and a bit of stubble on his jaw. A tight black v-neck t-shirt clung to every one of his muscles, showing off his tattooed arms nicely. Baggy ripped jeans hung from his narrow waist, and a pair of sneakers finished the look, both of which I knew had to cost more than the average commission I earned on a painting, despite their grungy appearance. Silver rings adorned several of his fingers, and a large, expensive-looking silver watch was on his left wrist. He looked up at me with a half-grin as he extended one hand, holding a single beautiful sunflower in a vase.

He was saying something, but I couldn't tear my eyes away from him, even to take the flower from his hand. He looked incredible, and I found myself wishing I could run my hands over his muscular arms, kiss my way from his jawline down his chest, even further down —

"Callie?" he asked, finally interrupting my thoughts. I felt my face flush as I shook my head, meeting his gaze.

He shot me a cocky grin; he probably knew exactly what I'd been thinking. I gathered my composure and took the sunflower from his hand as he leaned in for a quick hug. God, he smelled so good. Like sandalwood, tobacco, and vetiver — earthy and spicy. My pulse quickened as his fingers grazed my arm.

"Hi," I said with a small smile. I instinctively smelled the sunflower, although they don't really smell like anything at all. I admired it as Ace moved past me into the house. "Thanks for the sunflower; you remembered."

"You said it was your favorite. How could I forget that?" he asked, cocking his head at me, the corners of his mouth lifting.

Flustered, with a thousand butterflies swirling in my stomach, I sat the vase on the coffee table. I turned to face him, trying to think of something to say that would sound intelligent after being caught ogling him just now. His expression had turned serious, and with two large strides in my direction, he was in front of me, his hands on my waist.

My breath caught in my throat as he gazed at me. I was mesmerized, drowning in the pools of his bright blue eyes. He searched me with his stare, and after a few moments, he must have found what he was looking for. His lips were on mine, softly at first. When I responded by parting my lips and kissing him back, I felt his hands slide around my waist and up my back as the kiss deepened. I couldn't help it. A slight moan escaped me as his tongue found mine. A jolt of heat surged through me, going straight to my core while I let my hands roam up his muscled arms and shoulders.

Finally, Ace broke away, pulling back to give me a smoldering look, one side of his lips quirking up into a sly grin. "Hi," he said simply.

"Hi," I repeated breathlessly, no longer caring if I sounded intelligent or not. I was grinning at him like an idiot when the timer went off in the kitchen. I gasped. "The lasagna. I'll be right back."

I almost ran to the kitchen while trying to compose myself. I grabbed a potholder and pulled the lasagna out of the oven, relieved to see it looked perfect. I sat it down on a trivet and flinched when I felt arms snaking around me. I relaxed and smiled, turning my head a bit to see Ace behind me. "What are you doing? I told you I'd be right back."

"I thought you might need a little help." His warm breath against my ear sent shivers through my body while his hands found their way over my stomach. He planted kisses down my neck, gently and slowly, while one of his hands rucked up the fabric of my dress in front and dived under the lace of my panties.

I gasped as his fingers found me, pulling aside the flimsy material as he slid one long digit over my folds. He found my most sensitive spot, working it in a circular motion while heat slashed through my core. I grabbed the kitchen counter in front of me with both hands while he continued to work, nuzzling my neck with soft kisses as he did.

"God, you're so beautiful, Callie," he whispered against my neck, his breath setting my skin ablaze. His voice, so deep with that southern accent, was enough to melt me into a puddle.

I closed my eyes, letting my head fall back onto his shoulder while his fingers dipped inside of me. His other hand slid up to cup my breast, kneading it through the fabric of my dress.

"Ace…" I sighed, biting my lip. As he pulled me closer to him, I felt him growing hard against my backside. Fire surged through my veins as he continued this exquisite torture, the pressure building within me until I didn't think I could take it anymore.

He kissed my neck, nipping at my skin slightly with his teeth. "Come for me, baby."

That was all it took. With one final thrust of his fingers inside of me, I came apart. I reached back to grasp his thigh with one hand while steadying myself against the counter with the other. A moan slipped from my lips as he caught my mouth with his, kissing me hard while wringing the last of my orgasm out of me. Finally, I relaxed against him, his arms wrapping around me gently to keep me upright.

I was still panting, my heart still racing, when I turned to face him. A lazy smile spread across my face. "I didn't know you were so good in the kitchen." I let my hand slide down to the front of his jeans to stroke his hard length.

He grinned, placing a gentle kiss on my lips while pausing my hand with his. "We'll get to that later, baby. We can't let the lasagna get cold."

I laughed. "Are you serious?"

"Yeah, you made it, and I don't want to spoil it. I couldn't resist a little taste of dessert first, though," he said with a wink, which made my heart flip in my chest. He pulled me in close to whisper in my ear, "We have all night for that. If that's what you want."

I pulled back to look up into his eyes, smiling devilishly. "I definitely want dessert."

Ace

AFTER DINNER, CALLIE AND I RELAXED ON HER COUCH IN front of the television. God, it had been so difficult to stop her earlier in the kitchen, but really, I had just wanted to make her feel good and put her at ease. I could tell when I walked in tonight that she was strung pretty tightly, nervous about how things would go. I knew that because I was feeling the same way, and when I looked into her eyes, I could see it. We were attracted to each other, no denying it. It was time to stop trying to deny it.

I sat back against the plush cushions, draping my arm across the back of the couch. Callie snuggled into the crook of my arm, and I marveled at how perfectly we fit together.

She had the remote and was flipping through channels when I noticed the DVDs on the coffee table.

"Is that 'Bright Star?' The movie about John Keats?" I asked, nodding at the case on top of the stack. It was a movie based on the last three years of the poet's life and his love affair with Fanny Brawne. Keats was one of my favorite poets and I'd heard about the movie but hadn't seen it. I leaned up to grab the case, flipping it over in my hand to read the synopsis on the back cover.

I glanced back at Callie, who was staring at me in awe. "Yeah… you know Keats?"

I cast a wide grin her way, then started to recite the poem, which was the movie's namesake.

"Bright star, would I were stedfast as thou art —
Not in lone splendour hung aloft the night
And watching, with eternal lids apart,
Like nature's patient, sleepless Eremite,
The moving waters at their priest-like task."

Her eyebrows shot up as I spoke, her mouth forming a small 'o' shape. "Wow, I had no idea, Ace. I'm impressed!" she said when I finished. "When did you get into poetry?"

I shrugged, placing the DVD case back on the coffee table. "In high school, we had to read some poetry for English class, and it didn't completely suck. I checked out a poetry book from the school library. It had this poem by Keats in it, and it hooked me. I write a little myself, now and then."

She cocked her head at me, a smile playing on her full lips. She sat up a little straighter, looking at me with admiration. "Really? I'd love to read something you've written sometime."

I chuckled, leaning back once again while putting my arm around her. "I said I wrote a little. I didn't say it was any good."

"Oh, come on, I'm sure it's great. You saw my unfinished painting; it's only fair," she said, teasing while swatting at my chest. This easy banter with her was making me feel all sorts of ways, making me feel confident and crazy enough to think maybe I could share a stanza or two with her.

I turned to meet her deep blue gaze, still full of wonder and waiting for me to decide if I'd share my writing with her or not. The corners of my mouth lifted as I reached for my phone. "Only for you, Callie," I said, pulling up my notepad app to look for the one I wanted to read to her.

Her touch, a remedy, healing me
Her gaze, a bolster, strengthening me
Her kiss, a shield, protecting me
Unworthy, undeserving, unremarkable
Yet she sees something in me
Worthy, deserving, remarkable
Loveable

I stopped, glancing up at her for a reaction. I winced, thinking maybe this had been a mistake. I didn't know if it was any good by anyone's standard for poetry. It was just what I had written. How I was feeling at the time about her. And I wanted her to like it.

To my amazement, she was staring at me with a smile playing on her beautiful lips, one hand on her chest. I shot her a shy half-grin.

"It's beautiful, Ace."

She took my hand, pulling me closer, catching my lips with hers. I dropped the phone, letting it clatter to the floor by the couch as I turned my body towards hers, leaning into her touch. Her hands slid up my arms and shoulders while she deepened the kiss, parting her lips to me. My tongue met hers, both of us exploring with a frenzy fueled by desire.

Callie stretched back on the couch, her hands at the nape of my neck, guiding me to follow her. I shook my head, placing one hand on her forearm. At her questioning and disappointed gaze, I scooped her up into my arms. I'd be damned if the first time I tasted her was on her couch in front of the television, like a couple of high school kids fucking while the parents were out.

"Ace!"

That beautiful laugh of hers bubbled up out of her as I carried her up the stairs, where I presumed her bedroom would be. I was right; it was the only room upstairs, as a matter of fact. A king-sized bed covered in blankets and pillows sat beneath a large, half-circle window. There was a desk with various art paraphernalia strewn over it, and a large easel holding her sunflower painting stood beside it. The lights were off, yet moonlight streamed in through the large window to light my way to the bed, which also allowed us a gorgeous view of the Nashville night sky.

I felt her breathing grow shallow and fast as I held her against my chest. I looked down to see her gazing at me with a look I'd never seen before on her face. I wasn't sure what it was, but I liked it, and it stirred a warmth in my chest and a twitch in my cock.

Gently, I stood her at the foot of her bed, devouring her with my gaze. Our eyes locked while I pushed the straps of the yellow dress down her shoulders. She shimmied a bit, letting the dress fall to the floor around her feet. She stood before me in only a few scraps of lace that barely passed for underwear. My cock stirred again as I spotted her hardened nipples through the flimsy fabric.

"Wait," she said, grasping my forearm. "Do you have a condom?"

I shook my head, cursing myself. Why the fuck didn't I bring anything with me? But I knew I was fine; Dad had sent me for a physical when I started working at Dalton Enterprises, and I'd tested negative for everything. Plus, I hadn't been with anyone since that night at Indigo with Becky, and I'd used a condom then.

"No, but I'm all clear. I promise. Do you trust me?"

She pursed her lips in thought, then nodded. "Yeah, I do. I am, too. And on the pill."

Her eyes never leaving mine, she reached behind herself, unclasping the strapless bra, letting it fall to the floor to join the dress. She quickly stepped out of the skimpy panties as well, leaving her completely naked before me.

"You're fucking beautiful," I breathed, stepping back to appreciate the view.

She bit her lip, reaching out to tug on the waist of my jeans. "Your turn."

I raised an eyebrow and shot her a grin of encouragement. She tugged on the black shirt I wore, pulling it over my head. I tossed it to the side, where it narrowly missed landing on the easel. She made quick work of the button and zipper on my jeans, slowly dragging them down, along with my underwear. She kneeled before me, placing one hand around the base of my dick. Wrapping her lips around me, letting her tongue tease me. I moved to grip a handful of her hair, not taking my eyes off of that beautiful mouth of hers.

She moaned, making my whole body vibrate, her eyes closing as she worked. I didn't know how much longer I could last as she applied more pressure around my thickness. While she continued licking, sucking, torturing me—I knew I needed to be inside of her.

"Baby, get on the bed," I said, gently pulling her up by her arms. Reluctantly, she released me, doing as I asked. Callie laid back onto the bed, spreading her legs wide in invitation, her eyes darkened with desire, her core glistening with moisture. I moved over her, my cock nudging against her skin as I kissed my way up her body. The moonlight flooding into the room from the large window made her pale skin glow, urging me to touch every inch of her. The sudden need I had to be inside her stilled as I moved over her clit. I ran my tongue against her folds, tasting her, making her hips buck under me.

"You taste like heaven," I said before returning my mouth to her core. Her fingers tangled into my hair, holding me in place, as if I wanted to go anywhere else.

"Oh my God, Ace. Don't stop."

She made glorious moaning and sighing sounds while I continued stroking her with my tongue, finding her opening, dipping inside, exploring every hidden part of her. She moved her hips, meeting every thrust while the pressure built within us both. Our bodies were covered in sweat, our pulses racing, our breathing quick and shallow. I knew she was close.

"Come for me, Callie," I said, my voice husky against her core as I continued working her nub with my tongue.

"Ace!" She shattered into a million pieces as she came, her legs trembling on either side of me. I ran my hands over the skin of her thighs, slick with a sheen of sweat, as she came down.

I moved up her body, blazing a trail of kisses as I went. My cock throbbed, begging me for release. But I wasn't finished with her yet. I needed to know every part of her gorgeous body intimately. I stopped at each of her full tits, licking and sucking each nipple until they peaked, and she squirmed beneath me. I glanced up to see her watching me, a lazy smile on her face made only more beautiful by the light of the moon.

"I need you, Ace," she whispered, gripping my biceps. I

wasn't finished exploring, but there would be more time for that later, I decided. I moved up to place a kiss on her lips, mine still glistening with her juices. My cock, rock hard and ready for release, found her entrance, and I kissed her hard as I pushed into her.

She gasped, and I stilled, allowing her a moment to adjust to my size before I moved. Her face took on a blissful look again, so I knew she was okay. I went slowly at first as she moved her hips in time with me, finding a rhythm. She felt so good, so wet, so tight. I thought I could come right then and there, but I held on, driving into her deeper and faster while she wrapped her legs around me, digging her heels into my ass.

She moaned, panting beneath me. I knew she was close again, but I was closer. I wanted us to fall apart in unison, so I held on.

"Come on, baby. Together this time. Are you ready?" I asked breathlessly, still thrusting into her with a relentless rhythm.

She ran her hands down my back, then dug her nails into my skin just above my ass. "I'm ready," she whispered, barely audible over my racing heart.

That was all I needed to hear. With a final few thrusts, we found our release together. I collapsed on top of her, still inside, with her arms around my neck.

CHAPTER 9

Ace

I tossed back the tumbler of whiskey on the bar in front of me, my second in the twenty minutes I'd been waiting. Becky was late, but I wasn't sure why that surprised me. I looked at my watch again, then at the door with a scowl. I glanced around the bar, which was mostly empty, thank God. Precisely why I'd picked it—on the outskirts of town, a dive where no one I knew would be caught dead. I hoped it would be the last time I'd have to meet up with her.

I waved to the bartender to bring me another drink. Probably wasn't a great idea, but fuck, why not. I was annoyed I was here, waiting on this bitch to show up so I could ply her with copious amounts of alcohol so she'd tell me every goddamned secret she knew about this case. But I kept thinking about Callie and our last date the other night.

Magic—the only word I had for it. We had a chemistry

that could not be denied, even if we'd wanted to. It had to be magic, because I felt like I was under her spell, entranced and enthralled. I wanted to know everything about her. I wanted to become intimately familiar with every curve of her body. I'd never felt this way about another woman before, and it felt incredible and insane at the same time.

After the amazing sex, we'd both fallen asleep in her bed, our limbs intertwined. It felt so natural to wake up to her lying next to me; it scared me a little. Good things like this didn't happen to me, and Callie was definitely a good thing. The best thing. So, I found myself waiting for the other shoe to drop, for something to ruin it. And I hoped to God that Becky would not end up being that shoe.

I picked up my phone and quickly sent a text to Callie before I could overthink it.

I can't wait to see you again.

It was true; I couldn't wait to see her again. I watched for a moment, but I didn't see the telltale dots light up to indicate she was typing, so I put the phone away.

I caught movement out of the corner of my eye and looked towards the door to see Becky coming in, her eyes roving over the few patrons in the bar, looking for me. A black leather mini skirt hugged her hips with a long-sleeved, skin-tight black bodysuit underneath. Black stilettos on her feet and a black clutch in her hand. She finally spotted me, giving me a broad smile. She headed towards me with a little wave of her clutch.

The bartender sat another drink in front of me, and I immediately tossed it back. She took the barstool next to mine, slinging her bag on the bar before drawing me in for a hug. I didn't hug her back; I sat still as a statue with a scowl on my face, waiting for her to finish.

"Babe, what's the deal with this place? Took me twenty

minutes to get here," she said, a look of disgust twisting her features. She glanced at the stool before sitting down and gave the other patrons a disdainful look before her gaze drifted back to me.

"What do you mean? I like it." I gave her a half-hearted smile and realized I would have to put more effort in than this if I planned to get any information out of her. I pulled a pack of smokes out of my jacket pocket and offered one to her, which she refused. I shrugged, shook one out of the pack, and lit up, taking a drag. The bartender gave me a side-eyed glance but didn't say shit about it. Yet another reason why I loved dive bars.

Becky raised an eyebrow but dismissed my comment. "So, what's up? I was happy to hear from you. I know things are tough right now with the lawsuit and all. How are y'all holding up?" She placed a hand on my forearm and gave me a concerned look. That was the opening I needed, and she'd handed it to me on a silver platter.

I sighed, running my free hand through my hair. I ashed my cigarette into my empty glass, then took another drag. "Not so good. Dad's really taking it hard. He's not in the best of health either, you know. We're pretty worried about him," I said, laying it on thick amid a cloud of smoke as I exhaled. *Take the bait, Becky.*

"Bless his heart. I'm so sorry this is taking such a toll on him. And you too," she cooed, stroking my arm. The bartender came by to take her order while she shifted herself a little closer to me on her barstool.

My stomach turned. I didn't want her hands on me. All I could think about was Callie and the way she moaned my name when I made her come the other night. What I wouldn't have given to be lounging on her couch with her right now, watching some stupid show on Netflix, instead of being here in this shitty bar with Becky. But I had no choice. I had approximately one day left to get Andre's money to him, which meant I needed to get Dad some usable information as soon as possible. I took a deep breath and motioned to the bartender to bring me another drink.

"Yeah. I just wish we could find out more about how this lawsuit started. Because honestly, we're not doing anything wrong at Dalton. I think if we could just explain how this fungus occurs naturally, maybe they would drop the case." I shrugged as I spoke, then took one last drag off my cigarette before putting it out.

Becky was silent for a moment, studying her red nails. I watched out of the corner of my eye as she bit her lip and glanced around this fine establishment as if someone she knew could be watching. I suppressed a smile; I was pretty sure I had her on the hook. Now I just had to wait to reel her in.

She took a deep breath, then leaned in closer to me. "I don't know if you realize it, but I work for Emery and Knight, the law firm who's handling the prosecution."

I feigned surprise. "Seriously? I didn't know that."

She shook her head in affirmation. "Yeah, babe. I didn't think you did. I didn't want to bring it up and make things awkward, but hearing how much it's affecting your dad is just so sad. I mean, I'm just a legal secretary for Mr. Knight, but I hear things sometimes…" she said, letting her voice trail off.

"Becky, I couldn't possibly ask you to compromise your position at the law firm," I said, holding one hand up. *Christ, this was almost too easy.*

"No, it's okay. I don't know much, but I'd like to help your family, if I can." She placed her hand on my thigh, giving it a gentle squeeze. I tried not to flinch. "I heard Mr. Knight talking to someone about a whistleblower who works at Dalton Enterprises. Apparently, this person contacted the environmental agency who is behind the lawsuit."

Now we were getting somewhere. This could be the information Dad needed. If only she could give me a name.

"A whistleblower? Wow… I wonder who it could be."

She shook her head, taking a drink from the glass the bartender had placed in front of her. "Don't know. I might be able to find out, but they usually keep information like that pretty confidential."

Okay, no name. But maybe it would be enough. I said a prayer that it would be because I needed that money now to get Andre off my ass.

My cell phone vibrated in my pocket, alerting me of a text. I took the phone out and glanced at the notification.

Callie: Me too. Tomorrow?

My heart squeezed, just seeing her name on my screen. I had to get out of here. "Becky, I'm so sorry. I have to go. It's Dad. He needs me," I said as I stood, throwing a few bills down on the bar next to my empty glass.

Her face fell. "Oh no, babe. We were just getting started. Should I come with you?" she asked, a glimmer of hope in her eyes.

"No," I blurted, then backpedaled. "No, but thank you for offering; that's sweet. I'll call you soon, okay?" I backed away from her, not really caring if she replied. I turned on one heel and headed for the door as fast as I could.

I IGNORED DAD'S SECRETARY WHEN SHE TRIED TO STOP me, striding right past her desk and into Dad's office. He sat there looking defeated, his head in his hands, with paperwork scattered all over his desk. I fought a smile that threatened to break out over my face, knowing I had some information that could possibly help.

"I'm sorry, Mr. Dalton," his secretary said, on my heels as I entered his office. She gestured towards me with a scowl.

"It's okay," he said, waving her off. She left, giving me one last disapproving look. He glanced up, a quizzical expression on his wrinkled face, as I sat in the guest seat across from him.

"I saw Becky yesterday." I propped one ankle on the opposite knee, waiting for him to ask what I'd found out.

He raised an eyebrow. "And?"

"There's a whistleblower. Someone who works for Dalton contacted the Environmental Council. They've been supplying them with the information they needed to sue." I threw him a cocky smile.

His eyes grew wide with realization. "Who?"

"She didn't know. But she's working on getting a name."

Dad let a huge sigh loose, then picked up a book from his desk and flung it across the room, narrowly missing my head. He had quite an arm for an old bastard.

"DAMN IT. I need a name, boy. I can't do anything without a name," he said, his voice losing steam near the end.

"I know, Dad. She's getting it. But since we have this lead and it's only a matter of time before Becky has the name for us, I thought you could go ahead and pay me." I met his gaze directly, although my heart hammered in my chest.

"No."

"What do you mean?" I asked, a pang of fear slicing through my chest. I was running out of time. In fact, time was technically up already. Andre's men would be coming after my ass at any moment if I didn't deliver soon.

"I mean no. This lead could go nowhere. When I have a name, you'll have your money." He stared me down from behind his desk, his wrinkled face looking paler than I remembered, his frame not as intimidating as it used to be.

I huffed in anger. "She'll probably have the name for me tomorrow. What's the big deal?"

"Then you'll get your money tomorrow. What does one day matter?" he asked. I rolled my eyes. One day mattered a hell of a lot more than he knew, but I couldn't tell him that. *Fuck.*

Dad turned an icy gaze on me. "Don't you get an attitude with me. Those were the terms of the agreement you laid out, son. When I have usable information, you get your money. Now, I have work to do." He waved a hand in dismissal while turning to the paperwork on his desk.

"Fine," I spat. I rose from the guest chair, glaring at him while he ignored me. I slammed the door on my way out.

Fuck. I had to go see Becky again. Guilt washed over me, along with anger and regret. I stopped in the hallway just past Dad's secretary's desk, running my hands through my hair. I punched the wall, leaving a dent in it. A few heads poked out of offices, so I kept moving. I strode towards the building's exit, making a beeline for my Jeep. I knew it was only a matter of time before Callie found out about what was going on. And with my history, she would automatically assume I've been fucking Becky this whole time. I couldn't blame her for that; I had a reputation. I pulled my phone out of my pocket, seeing her sunflower painting as my wallpaper. If I had any hope of salvaging this budding relationship with her, I had to come clean before she found out from someone else.

Callie

I CLOSED THE FRONT DOOR BEHIND GRAND-MÈRE, THEN leaned against it with a sigh. She'd just stopped by to bring me some fresh cookies she'd made and, of course, nonchalantly find out what has been going on with Ace. And that was the problem. Nothing.

He had texted me the other day to say he couldn't wait to see me again, and after I texted back to say, "Me too. Tomorrow?" he had never replied. I wasn't sure how to interpret that. The three dates Grand-Mère had paid for were complete now. Had he decided he wasn't interested anymore? Had he ever been interested at all? Maybe it was all a ploy to get me into bed. Well, mission fucking accomplished.

I leaned my head back, closing my eyes. My head kept thinking up all the worst-case scenarios, but my heart was telling me not to give up hope. The connection I felt with Ace seemed real. It had to be real. He wouldn't just ghost me now. He wouldn't.

I took the plate of cookies into the kitchen without touching them. I wasn't hungry. In spite of myself, I kept thinking about Ace's silence.

What if he's met someone else already? Someone he works with? Or maybe it's that Becky chick from Indigo? What if there's something about me he doesn't like? Maybe I'm too tall. Maybe I'm not thin enough. What if he's been playing me this whole time?

STOP.

I stood still in my kitchen, fists clenched at my sides, my eyes closed. I took several deep breaths to clear my mind. I had to stop. I reminded myself that it was all speculation at this point. It had only been a couple of days. There could be any number of reasons he hadn't texted me back yet. And besides, if he had been playing me, then fuck him. I would not waste time crying over another asshole ever again. *Get yourself together, Callie.*

Suddenly, the words from his poem resonated in my head. Worthy. Deserving. Remarkable. Loveable. He wrote those words; that's how I made him feel. He wasn't playing me. This was the real thing.

With one final deep breath, I decided I'd head upstairs to work on my sunflower painting. Working on a project always helped me clear my head, and that's exactly what I needed to do now.

I pulled out my palette along with a tube of paint and squeezed some Titanium White onto it. My phone trilled with a text message, so I reached into the back pocket of my jeans to retrieve it, a slow smile spreading over my face as I read.

Ace: Are you home now? I need to see you.

See, Callie? You idiot. I berated myself for thinking the worst only minutes ago. I put the palette down, my painting forgotten for now, to text him back.

Me: I am, come on over.

Ace

I ARRIVED AT CALLIE'S FRONT DOOR, RUBBING MY SWEATY palms on my jeans before knocking. I inhaled deeply, pursing my lips. I was about to tell her everything. The gambling and the money I owed to Andre, how his "collection agents" would soon be looking to extract an alternate form of payment from me. About Becky and how Dad wanted to use me to get information out of her about the lawsuit. And I wanted to tell Callie how I felt about her; how I'd never felt like this about another woman before in my life, and how it both excited me and scared the shit out of me at the same time.

And I hoped to hell she would believe that I was ready to change my life on my own terms. The old Ace was gone; a new Ace stood before her now, one who she helped create. I couldn't believe only a few short weeks ago I'd been at Indigo, blowing twenty thousand dollars on a poker game and fucking a chick I didn't even know in the bathroom. Fighting like hell against Dad because I didn't want to give that life up. But I didn't want that life anymore. I wanted Callie and a new life with her.

Shortly after I knocked, she opened the door, a bright smile on her gorgeous face. Her long, mahogany hair hung in loose waves, her deep blue eyes sparkling. She wore a light blue raglan t-shirt and ripped jeans that hugged her ass so tight I wished I could peel them off of her immediately.

"Hey, you," she said, holding the door open wider to allow me to slide past her. I tore my gaze from her long enough to enter the house, then turned back to meet her questioning eyes. My heart hammering in my chest. I searched for the right words to tell her everything I needed to say.

"Is something wrong?"

She motioned for me to join her on the couch in the small living room. So I did, rubbing my hands against my jeans once more. I took a deep breath.

"No. No, nothing's wrong. I just wanted to apologize for taking so long to text you back, and I wanted to—"

"It's so funny you mentioned that," she said, grinning sheepishly. She bit her lip and scrunched up her nose. "My imagination was running away with me only a few minutes before you texted me. So crazy, all the worst-case scenarios our minds can come up with, right?" she asked, shaking her head.

"What worst-case scenarios?" I asked both intrigued and using the question as a stalling tactic.

"Oh, you know. Stuff every girl thinks when the guy she likes doesn't text back right away. Maybe he's changed his mind. Or he's found someone else. Maybe he's been playing me this whole time," she said, meeting my eyes with that last example.

I could see there was still some worry there. *Maybe he's found someone else. Fuck.* Why hadn't I just texted her back the other day?

But wait.

"Wait, did you just admit that you like me?" I asked, rewinding her last words in my brain. "Because I think you did." I grinned, leaning back on the couch, momentarily forgetting what I'd come here for.

She rolled her eyes, a shy smile forming on her pouty lips. "I guess my secret is out. Yes, Ace Dalton. I kinda, sorta like you. A little bit. Okay? Happy now?" she asked, laughing. She rested one hand on my thigh, and my heart squeezed at her confession.

"Happy? I'm ecstatic. Best news I've heard all year, as a matter of fact."

I grinned like an idiot, taking her hand and pulling her towards me. She didn't resist and was soon lying against my chest on the couch, our faces only inches apart.

"The truth is, I'm falling for you, Ace. I'm falling hard." Her words were barely more than a whisper against my lips. She scanned my face for an acknowledgment, for some sign that I felt the same way. And that's when I knew.

I couldn't tell her about all the bullshit I came here to unload on her. The gambling, Becky, the collection agents,

Dad's schemes. It would break her heart, and I couldn't do that to her. Not when she'd just admitted she was falling for me the same way I was falling for her. I didn't want to fuck this up. Callie was the best thing to ever happen to me. Ever. And I wanted to be that guy she was falling for, more than anything. So, I would take care of this shit on my own, as quickly as possible.

I'd go to Becky and explain why it was so important for me to get that name from her immediately. As soon as I had it, I'd pass the information to Dad, and he'd give me the twenty grand I needed to pay Andre. I'd have Andre off my back, I'd tell Becky I have a girlfriend, and I'd continue working for Dad to prove to him I'm getting my shit together. All would be right in the world in just a few more days. So why should I tell Callie and risk breaking her heart? Risk having her tell me to go to hell, that she never wanted to see me again? I was one lucky bastard to have this gorgeous, talented, intelligent woman falling in love with me; it was best not to push my luck, I concluded.

I took her hand from my chest, raising it to my lips. I planted a slow, soft kiss on her palm. "I'm falling for you too, Callie."

Callie

ACE LIFTED ME INTO HIS ARMS AS IF I WEIGHED NOTHING, carrying me up the stairs towards my bedroom. We never broke our kiss. It only became more urgent and passionate with every step. He placed me on my feet near my bed, our hands roaming furiously over each other's clothes, fumbling with buttons and zippers until we were both completely naked.

The sun was on its way down, a fading golden light streaming into my room through the large half-circle window above the bed. As the sun made its descent towards the horizon, my sunflower painting resting on the easel in the corner caught my eye while Ace kissed his way down my neck to my collar bone. We'd just admitted how we felt about each other, that we were falling for one another. My painting made me think about the Greek myth I'd told Ace about, and for a split second, anxiety sliced through my heart.

Was I doomed to be the sunflower? Would I fall so deeply for Ace there would be no turning back? Would I spend the rest of my life in love with him, even if he decided one day that he didn't love me anymore? I moaned as his hands slid over my body, one of them finding my core, already soaking for him. A low growl resonated from his throat as he moved in slow circles over my most sensitive spot, still searing a path of kisses over my skin. I threw my head back and held on to him, deciding I didn't care anymore. I would be the sunflower for Ace, if that was my destiny.

He stopped, pulling me towards the bed. He motioned for me to get on the mattress, which I did. Then he was behind me with his arms curled around my waist. He whispered into my ear, "Put your hands up against the window. Don't move them."

Eagerly, I moved towards the head of the bed, on my knees with my hands up against the half-circle window. The sun had gone down now, so it was dark, but it was oddly thrilling to know I was completely on display. If I had neighbors, I might've been concerned about someone seeing me like this, stark naked, pressed up against the glass above my bed. I turned my head to see what Ace was doing when I felt the mattress dip below me. I gasped when I felt his tongue against my folds, licking softly up and down.

The glass was cold against my skin, the night air seeping through and causing goosebumps to rise on my flesh. My nipples were taut, pressed against the glass as I rode Ace's tongue. My hot breath fogged the glass while I panted, his tongue swirling over my clit as he slid two fingers inside me, pumping them in and out, hitting just the right spot. His other hand gripped my hip tightly, keeping me in place as I ground myself against his mouth and writhed against the window.

"Oh my God," I breathed, moving my hips in time with his tongue, keeping my hands up against the glass.

He moaned, sending a vibration through my core, setting fire to every cell in my body. A cold heat burned through me while the pressure continued to build. I moaned, sighed, and screamed his name while he worked me until I couldn't take it anymore.

"Get there, baby, come for me," he breathed against my skin, continuing the delicious torture he was inflicting on my body. My sweaty hands slid down the cold window as I obeyed, coming apart and letting myself go.

"Ace!" I screamed. I felt his hands on my thighs, fingers digging in deep as I came. I moved down from the window, my overheated body feeling the loss of the cool glass but more than ready to feel Ace inside of me.

I straddled him, his still hard cock nudging at my entrance. I slid myself over him, taking him all the way in as he gasped. His hands rested on my hips as I moved, slowly at first, enjoying the feel of him deep inside of me. His hips rose to meet mine as we found our rhythm, and I rode him hard. A sheen of sweat bloomed over my skin once again as I moved, throwing my head back, moaning his name.

"Baby, you feel so good," he groaned, his hands sliding up over my breasts, kneading each one, rolling my nipples between his fingers. He moved one hand between us, rubbing my clit as I moved, making me feel as if my core were on fire.

He gripped my hips, flipping me over onto my back in a fluid motion, then pounded into me with my legs over his shoulders. We cried out simultaneously, finding our release at the same time. He rolled to the side and gathered me to him, my back to his chest, his now spent cock resting against my ass. A lazy smile spread across my face as he kissed my neck, his fingers tracing circles on my hip.

Maybe we would be each other's sunflowers instead, I mused.

CHAPTER 10

Ace

"*D*amn," I muttered, noticing the low fuel light flashing on the dash of my Jeep. I'd just left Callie's house after a couple of rounds of mind-blowing sex. She had asked me to stay the night, but I had plans for the next day, and I wanted an early start and didn't want to have to explain myself to her. Since I'd decided not to share all the loose ends I was trying to tie up from my old life, I'd rather not have to lie to Callie about where I needed to be bright and early the next morning. So, I was headed back home—well, to my parents' house—to sleep for a few hours.

I pulled off on the next exit, seeing a glowing sign from the interstate for a gas station. I pulled in next to the pump and pulled my debit card out of my wallet, the only card I had now, which was attached to the checking account where my Dalton Enterprises paychecks were deposited. I would never admit it to Dad, but it felt kind of good to earn my own paychecks for a change.

I exited the vehicle, noticing how deserted the place was; there wasn't another customer in sight. I checked my watch. It was three in the morning. I could see a clerk inside the convenience store, wearing headphones and reading a book, bobbing her head to the music.

I swiped my card, then I removed the gas cap. I started the pump, setting it up so it would continue to pump automatically until the tank was full. Then I pulled my phone out. There was a text from Callie.

Callie: *Drive safely, call me tomorrow <kissy face emoji> <heart emoji>*

I smiled at the glowing screen, only half noticing as another car pulled into the pump behind me. I swiped to type a message back to her when I heard a car door open abruptly. I turned around to see a fist coming at my face. I was too slow to react; it made contact and the sickening sound of cracking cartilage seemed to echo in the empty lot.

My eyes began watering immediately, and my phone clattered to the ground as I groaned in pain. I opened one eye, squinting at my attacker… rather, attackers. *Oh, fuck.*

The collection agents. Andre wanted payment in full. Now.

One guy moved behind me to hold my arms behind my back. The other guy, the one who had just broken my nose, threw several more punches at me. My face, my stomach, then kicked me in the balls. Bones cracked, blood splattered, and I hissed, groaned, and cursed with every blow he dealt. I tried to pull my arms loose, but the guy held me tight. Each of them had at least a hundred pounds and several inches on me. I was no match for either of them, but put them together? A snowball in hell had a better chance than I did.

"Please, let me talk to Andre," I said between punches, blood seeping from my split lips.

"The time for talking is over, Dalton," the one holding me growled. The other one threw a few more punches before my legs gave out. The guy holding me finally let go, allowing me to smack the pavement beside my Jeep face first.

He issued a few kicks to my side, my ribs cracking audibly before he backed away. My eyes were swollen. I felt blood trickling down my face, pooling on the ground. My head felt like it was three times its normal size, not to mention how my stomach, ribs, and balls felt after enduring the punishment Andre's goons had dished out. I pushed up with the palms of my hands, but it was no use. I allowed myself to flop back onto the ground with a hiss.

The one who'd been punching me ran a hand through his hair and adjusted his sleeves. "Boss said that's your last warning. You have twenty-four hours before we extract final payment."

The one who'd been holding my arms landed a hard kick in my side as he walked past. They climbed back into their black SUV, driving away as if nothing ever happened. I watched the taillights disappear onto the interstate from where I laid next to my Jeep and heard the gas pump shut off, indicating the tank was now full.

My phone was a few feet away, partially under the vehicle. I groaned, pulling myself towards it until my fingers brushed the edge of the phone. I managed to dig a fingernail into the edge of the case, dragging it towards me. The exertion of just retrieving my phone had my already throbbing head spinning and threatening to blackout. I squinted, trying to see the screen through the blood and sweat that dripped down my brow. It was no use, so I held the home button until a robotic voice asked how it could help me.

"Call Jasper," I said with a ragged breath. As the phone started ringing, I turned my face towards the convenience store again, where the clerk still sat in the window, reading with her headphones on.

Callie

I OPENED MY EYES AFTER SAYING A SILENT PRAYER, ONLY to see that Ace was still unconscious. Lying in the hospital bed, covered with a white sheet and blanket, needles and tubes in his arms, he looked so vulnerable. *How the fuck did this happen?*

After leaving my place, he was headed home to get some rest. He said he had something important to take care of the next morning. Then I got a phone call from his brother, Jasper, around lunchtime today, letting me know that Ace had been beaten up badly the night before and was in the hospital and unconscious. Jasper only knew to call me because Ace's phone was still in his hand when they found him, and my text was the first thing on the screen when Jasper turned it on. As far as I knew, we still didn't know who did this or why. Maybe it was random, or perhaps someone had tried to mug him? I had no clue. I was just glad he was still alive.

I'd been here all day; I rushed over as soon as I hung up with Jasper. The doctor had been here when I arrived, talking to Ace's brothers. Apparently, Ace had suffered multiple broken ribs, a broken nose, and several lacerations on his face and body, but the doctor seemed to think he would be okay. His body just needed time to rest, and he would wake up when he was ready.

It was getting late; I hadn't had lunch or dinner because I didn't want to leave his side in case he woke up. Ace's mother had been here briefly, and Jasper and Nick, but none of them stayed. I didn't want him to wake up all alone.

I moved to sit on the edge of his bed, taking his hand in mine. I traced the lines of his tattoos on his hands and forearms, moving carefully around the needles, studying them through blurry eyes. I blinked back tears, then glanced at his face, so still and somber.

Could he hear me? I moved closer so I could whisper in his ear, just in case he could. "Ace, it's Callie. I'm here and I'm not leaving. Rest and get better, but wake up soon for me, okay?" I bit back a sob, squeezing his hand as I spoke. There was no recognition on his face, no sign he'd heard me, but I believed he did.

An idea occurred to me. I pulled out my phone, then tapped on the screen until I found what I was looking for. A poetry website, where I found some poems by John Keats. I held his hand and read a few of them until the nurse came in to check his IV. She gave me a sad smile while she took his vitals, patting me on the shoulder as she left. She returned a few minutes later with a tray of hospital food for me, a blanket, and a pillow. Her kindness brought tears to my eyes once again.

After reading another poem to Ace and forcing myself to eat a few bites of food, I curled up in the uncomfortable reclining chair by his bed, pulling the blanket around myself. I watched his face until I fell asleep, hoping to see some sign of him coming out of his slumber, but there was none.

Ace

"FUCK," I GROANED, OPENING MY EYES AND DRAGGING the word out. Everything fucking hurt. I looked around in confusion at the hospital bed, the tubes in my arms, and the empty room furnished with flowers and cards, when it all started coming back to me.

The gas station. Andre's men. The still unpaid debt. *Shit*.

I ran a hand over my face and winced. I felt scabbed over cuts on my forehead, my cheeks, and my lips. My nose was covered with a splint and there was gauze inside each nostril. I glanced down and saw a light blue hospital gown. Purple bruises mingled with the tattoos on my arms, and when I leaned up to take a better look at my legs, a sharp pain erupted in my side, which made me gasp. I pulled the gown up to reveal more cuts and bruises on my shins. I carefully laid back on the mattress with a sigh, suddenly exhausted.

Wait, how long had I been here? That thought sent a rush of anxiety and fear through me. Where was everyone? Where was Callie? What had Andre done? My eyes searched the room for my phone, not finding it anywhere. Where the hell could it be?

I moved again to get out of bed; I had to find my phone. I had to make sure Callie was okay. I groaned as I pulled the IV needle out of my arm. It hurt, but it was nothing compared to everything else. My entire body was one giant throbbing wound, and I panted as I stood on shaky legs, feeling faint. I spotted a cabinet by what appeared to be the bathroom door, so I headed in that direction, slowly navigating the short distance between my bed and the closet, each step more painful than the last. Every breath I took made my ribs ache while spots swam in my vision, threatening to pull the plug on this expedition at any moment.

Finally, I reached it, grasping the handle like it was a lifesaver. I pulled it open to see my dirty, torn clothing in a clear bag, with my shoes sitting next to it. And right on top were my wallet and my phone.

I grabbed the phone, feeling lightheaded. No way was I going to make it back to that bed right now. Halfway between my current location and the bed was one of those weird sleeper recliners, and I figured I could make it there before I collapsed. I clutched the phone to my chest while slowly making my way there, then sat down as gently as I could while every cell in my body screamed in protest.

I leaned back, trying to catch my breath, and turned the phone on. The battery was at 12%, and I had no charger, so I had to make this quick. There were a few text messages, but I ignored them as I searched for Callie's name. Then I noticed an unknown number had sent a text. A chill ran down my spine as I clicked on it.

Tick tock.

That's all it said, but I knew who it was from. *Fuck*.

9%.

I kept scrolling through messages from Jasper, Nick, Mom, even Becky, until I found Callie's unanswered text I'd seen when Andre's men jumped me at the gas station. I struggled to keep my eyes focused as I typed.

R u ok

I looked at the calendar app while I waited for a reply. Three days. I'd been here for three days. What had Andre done while I was out of it?

I went back to Callie's text and didn't see any dots to indicate she was typing. Fear and anger fought for control as I stared at the phone. If he'd done something to her, I would kill him.

I would kill him.

Fuck. 6%.

139

Come on, Callie, answer me.

I closed my eyes, willing her to reply before my phone died. I had to know she was okay. If Andre had hurt her because of me, I swear—

"Babe! You're awake!"

My eyes flew open. Standing in front of me, her eyes wide with a smile that stretched from ear to ear on her face, was Callie, holding a takeout bag. She looked like a mother-fucking angel to me. Relief washed over me, so much that I lost my grip on the phone, letting it fall to the linoleum floor.

She rushed to my side, the smile fading from her beautiful face. God, I'd never been so happy to see someone in my life. She was here, she wasn't hurt, she was perfect and gorgeous, and she was here.

"Nurse! I need a nurse in here!" she yelled, looking at me with concern as she knelt by me, dropping the bag on the floor next to my chair. "I'm so sorry I wasn't here when you woke up, babe," she said. Her eyes brimmed with tears as she squeezed my hand.

"Thank God you're okay," I breathed, squeezing her hand in return.

She gave me a confused smile, shaking her head. "Of course I'm okay."

Two nurses came bustling in, so Callie released me and moved back to let them work. They each took an arm and heaved me up out of the chair. We trudged back to the bed where they helped me lay down gently, though I still gasped and winced at the pain. One nurse gave me a disapproving look as she set to work, putting the IV back in my arm. I closed my eyes, ignoring her.

She's okay. She's okay. I repeated to myself, over and over, while the nurse fussed over me. But fuck, I still owed Andre. She wasn't safe, not with me.

I opened my eyes to see her standing there, eyes wide as she watched the nurse work. She gave me a tentative smile while she chewed on a fingernail. Those tantalizing lips. Those gorgeous blue eyes. That rich, brown hair cascading over her shoulders. That beautiful soul.

I wanted to throw something. I wanted to hurl my phone against the wall and scream. I'd been trying to get my shit together all this time, and still, I was going to fuck it all up with her. I had to, to keep her safe. I still owed Andre, and he wasn't going to stop until I paid him, one way or another. I hoped to hell he didn't know about Callie yet. I had to make sure he never knew about her and what she meant to me. If he hurt her, or worse—I couldn't let that happen.

I wouldn't let that happen.

Callie

I watched as the nurses transported Ace back to his bed and re-connected his IV while he winced in pain. I bit my lip, wanting to do something to help but knowing I'd only be in the way if I tried. He gave me a withering glance, then closed his eyes while the one remaining nurse took his vitals and double-checked the reinstated IV.

She shook her head at him. "Please stay put, Mr. Dalton. You need your rest." Before heading out the door, she gave me a pointed look as if telling me to make sure he did. I nodded in agreement as she closed the door behind her, then moved to Ace's bedside.

I sat on the mattress beside him and smoothed a hand over his disheveled curls. "I should've been here when you woke; the nurses kept telling me to go get something to eat, that you'd be fine. I shouldn't have listened to them."

"No, it's fine. Don't feel bad." He shook his head, his breath still a bit ragged. He gave me a tired smile, then glanced away.

"What were you doing out of bed, anyway?" I asked, my brows knitting together. I recalled seeing his phone in his hands when I walked in. I glanced around and caught sight of it underneath the reclining sleeper chair I'd been using.

"It doesn't matter. Callie..." he started, his voice hitching on my name. He finally met my gaze again, a pained look in his eyes.

I panicked. "What's wrong? Should I get the nurse?" I reached for the button next to his bed to ring a nurse. He grabbed my hand, stopping me.

"I don't need a nurse." He stopped speaking and stared into my eyes for a long moment. A ball of fear and anxiety quickly formed in the pit of my stomach, making me feel nauseous.

"Ace... what's wrong?"

I knew what he was going to say as the question fell from my lips. I had known it all along.

"This isn't going to work, Callie."

I felt as if the wind had been knocked out of me. My eyes stung, and an iciness settled over my heart. "What do you mean?"

He closed his eyes, leaning his head back onto the pillow while one hand went to his forehead. "You know what I mean. Please, don't make me spell it out."

I did know. I knew exactly what he meant.

He and I weren't going to work, and I had always known that truth, from the moment I saw him and had felt an irrational pull towards him. How could we ever work out long term? Ace was trying to change, but could a tiger ever change its stripes? He was everything I had sworn off after Vic, but I'd let myself be persuaded, let myself fall under his spell. I had been incredibly stupid, and now my heart would pay the price. Again.

I crossed my arms over my chest, my pulse racing as I tried to hold back my tears. "Did I misunderstand the other night? You said you were falling for me. What the fuck happened, Ace?" My voice was getting louder, and I couldn't stop myself from asking those questions. I felt betrayed—by him, by my own heart, by this fucking idea of love in general. Blood rushed to my cheeks as anger rose up in me alongside the hurt.

He stayed silent, pursing his lips and looking away from me.

"Look at me! I deserve an explanation!"

I was met with more silence. I saw his chest quaking, saw a tear rolling down his cheek while he stared out the window. Finally, he spoke, his voice hoarse and tired. "There's no explanation that's good enough, Callie. I'm a fuck up. Always have been, always will be."

"That's a goddamn excuse. Why can't you just tell me why the sudden change of heart?"

Realization struck me. I shook my head, putting one hand to my mouth. "But it's not sudden, is it? You've felt this way the whole time, haven't you?"

He winced as if I'd physically struck him. A part of me was glad I was making him uncomfortable, making him face how he was destroying me.

"Callie... please."

I barked a laugh. "Please? You've got some fucking nerve." I strode over to the desk where my bag laid before turning back to him. "I knew this was going to happen. I knew you would break my heart if I gave it to you. Thanks for proving me right."

I glared at him as I grabbed my purse and headed for the door. I stopped short, turning to face him, against my better judgment. His face was wet with tears, twisted into a picture of grief and regret. Was I supposed to care? *Fuck this and fuck him.*

I palmed the handle of the door and found it was opening up in my direction already. A pretty blonde wearing a skimpy mini dress with loosely drawn laces on the bodice, revealing most of her breasts, stood before me. Her red lips formed a surprised little "o" when she met me at the door, stopping her short.

"Oh hey, babe," she said, glancing past me to Ace. "I just heard, got here as soon as I could." She turned her blue eyes on me again, giving me a once over with a raised eyebrow. "Am I interrupting something?"

I shook my head, choking out a bitter laugh. I looked at Ace, whose face was ashen as he stared at the two of us.

It was Becky from Indigo. The girl he'd fucked in the bathroom without even knowing her name.

He'd been playing me this whole time.

"No. I was just leaving." With one final glance at Ace, my heart detonated, shattering into a billion tiny pieces. I strode past her, pausing briefly before exiting the room.

"He's all yours."

CHAPTER 11

Ace

"*Y*ou need to eat something."

I turned to face Mother, her perfect brows drawn together, her thin lips pursed. She nodded to a tray on the coffee table where a now lukewarm bowl of chicken soup sat, untouched. I said nothing. I was empty and broken. I had nothing left to say, nothing left to give.

She sighed, getting up from the wingback chair next to mine, pausing to pat my shoulder. "Please try to eat something soon, okay? For me?" She leaned down to brush a kiss against my cheek before exiting the room.

I stared out the window again. It was overcast; it looked like it might rain. A perfect reflection of my heart.

It had been a week since Callie left my hospital room. A week since my black heart had shriveled up, turning into an empty, withered shell inside my chest. I'd been released since then and had made my parents' library my personal domain, where I could stew in my own misery in private. Except for the daily intrusions from Mother begging me to eat or let her walk me outside for some fresh air. I always refused. I was empty and broken now. I had nothing left.

The only thing keeping me going now was worry. I checked social media at regular intervals to see if Callie had been online or had posted anything. Upon seeing a recent "like" on her friend Sarah's latest post, or seeing that she had been online thirty-two minutes ago, my mind was put at ease. For the time being.

I had to believe that what I had done would keep her safe. That pushing her away, in the worst possible way, would keep her safe from Andre. I'd get the money for him soon, and then she'd be safe for good, although what I'd done could never be forgiven. I'd lost her forever, but as long as she stayed alive, I could accept that the rest of my life would be a living hell.

I closed my eyes, tired of looking at the gray sky, and let those last few moments replay in my mind for the millionth time. When I'd broken her goddamned heart. It had been bad enough, would have been hard enough to live with. Then Becky's ass had to show up and make it worse. Fucking Becky. I'd thrown her out as soon as Callie left. I slammed my fist against the arm of the chair. If only I'd come clean to Callie that night about everything. But I'd chosen not to, and in classic Ace style, I'd fucked everything up.

"Hey, bro." My eyes opened at the soft greeting. Jasper had quietly entered the library and had taken the seat previously occupied by Mother. He looked at me with worried eyes, leaning forward in the chair with his elbows propped on his knees, hands clasped in front of him. He was the very picture of the perfect son; well-dressed, clean-shaven, bright, and cheerful. The polar opposite of me.

I took a deep, ragged breath. "I'm not in the mood for company, Jas."

"Okay. I just wanted to let you know, you don't have to worry about Andre anymore. It's been taken care of." He moved to rise from the chair, but I raised a hand, stopping him.

"Wait. 'Taken care of?'"

He nodded. "I couldn't risk them coming back to finish the job, Ace. I put two and two together after what you told me that night when I found you drunk at the bar. Nick and I paid Andre what you owed him. You can pay us back whenever. It's done. And I hope you won't get into a situation like that again."

I exhaled a ragged breath, scrubbing my face with one hand, feeling the cuts from that night that were still healing. I didn't know whether to be insanely grateful to my brothers because now I knew Callie would be safe from Andre's men, or whether I should be insanely pissed off that they handled my shit for me without even asking me first.

"What the fuck, Jasper?" I leaned back, putting both hands over my face. Damn it, I was going to take care of it. I had a plan, although it was taking longer than expected and had nearly gotten me killed in the process — not to mention it had put Callie's life on the line. But Callie was safe now, no matter how irrationally angry I was at my brothers for cleaning up my mess. In the end, her safety was all that really mattered.

"You would've done the same for either of us. I know you would have."

"Fuck. I'll pay you back, I swear," I said, shaking my

head, still in disbelief. It didn't really surprise me that Jasper had done this, but Nick… I was a little shocked, to be honest. That hardass cared about me after all. Who fucking knew?

"I'm not worried. I know where to find you if you don't." He shot me a soft smile before standing up. "Oh, I met Callie while you were out of it."

Just hearing her name hurt. "Oh, yeah?" I asked, not about to go into all of that shit with Jasper right now. I could barely stand the replay in my own head, much less having to say it out loud to another human being.

"She's a hell of a woman. Crazy about you too, God only knows why." He laughed while I felt like I'd just been shot through the heart. "Try not to fuck that up, Ace." And with that, he was gone.

Too late.

Callie

I MUSTERED UP A WEAK SMILE WHEN I OPENED THE DOOR to let Sarah in, along with a pizza and twelve-pack of beer. I wasn't in the mood to entertain her, but she wouldn't take no for an answer. At least I'd talked her into coming to my place instead of meeting at a bar so I could stay in my pajamas with my hair in a messy bun.

It had been one long week since I'd left Ace's hospital room. I'd spent it analyzing everything he had ever said to me, right from the beginning, looking for clues I'd missed before. How had I been so blind? Why had I given in to my attraction to him when I had known where it would lead?

"Hey, girl," Sarah sang, stretching the word "girl" out. She moved past me to deposit the beer and pizza on the coffee table before turning to wrap me in an enormous hug. I patted her back half-heartedly.

"Hey, babe," I said, my tone despondent.

She pulled back to give me a once over, holding me at arm's length. "I knew it was bad, but I didn't know it was this bad, Cal. Tell me."

I dropped to the couch, immediately putting my head in my hands. She sat next to me and placed a hand on my shoulder. Tears had been waiting just under the surface, ready to fall at a moment's notice. Now I felt them rolling down my cheeks, and I didn't even try to stop them. Maybe if I kept crying, eventually I'd run out of tears, and I could finally forget about Ace.

"Oh, babe," Sarah crooned, rubbing my shoulder while I sobbed. I leaned against her, letting her wrap one arm around me. "What happened?"

I sniffled, wiping my cheeks with my fingers. "It was all a lie. He played me, Sarah."

She frowned. "What? I thought it was going so well?"

I shook my head. "Yeah, it was. Until it wasn't."

"Just tell me if I need to murder him for you," she asked, still holding me.

In spite of myself, I laughed. "No need for murder, although I appreciate the offer. I need you, can't have you going to prison."

"Okay, I get that. But the offer still stands, babe. Now, spill it."

She smoothed my hair back behind my ear as I thought about where to begin. I honestly didn't feel like going over it all, especially the last few moments in Ace's hospital room when he'd told me things weren't working out between us and when Becky showed up. I felt like a fool; I didn't want Sarah to think I was one, too.

But I needed to get it out. Maybe that was the key to moving on, and I didn't have many people I could talk to. Grand-Mère would only feel guilty about winning the dates with Ace at the bachelor auction if I told her everything. I'll have to tell her eventually that things didn't work out, but maybe I could spare her the details and the guilt. Sarah was my best bet for catharsis, so I took a deep breath and started talking.

I started at the beginning and told her everything, including how I resisted him at first and how he'd won me over with his charm. How we'd grown closer with every date, every text message, every phone call. How he made me feel like no one else ever has. Special, beautiful, intelligent. Then I thought of his poem, the one he wrote for me.

Worthy, deserving, remarkable. Loveable.

Was the poem a lie, too? Did he even write it for me? Those four words described exactly how he made me feel, and fresh tears spilled onto my cheeks as I told the story. Yet another tragic love story for me. When would I get my happy ending?

I was on my third beer by the time I finished up with the hospital room scene, telling Sarah about Becky showing up and my realization that I'd been played for a fool all along. I felt emotionally spent after reliving it, and I had a pretty good buzz going, too.

Sarah shook her head, giving me a commiserating look. "Are you sure you don't want me to kill him?"

"Put your knife away." I laughed and took a pull from my beer. Although telling the story to Sarah was hard, I had to admit I felt like a weight had been lifted from my shoulders. I felt somewhat better now that I had someone to sympathize with me and who wanted to commit murder on my behalf. That's what friends were for, right?

"Fine," she said, rolling her eyes and waving a hand in dismissal. "We have to plan your next move, anyway." She raised an eyebrow at me while taking a bite of the now cold pizza.

"My next move?"

"Yes! You have to show him you're fine. That your life is not over now. You can and will move on without him!" She paused for dramatic effect before adding, "Living your best life is the best revenge, babe."

My next move. I hadn't thought any further ahead than what to have for dinner most days recently. I didn't even know I needed to have a "next move," much less what it should be.

"I don't know…" I said, trailing off. I wrinkled up my nose as I thought. What I really wanted to do was lie in bed for the next six months with the covers pulled up over my head. But I couldn't do that. I had clients waiting for paintings, and I had Grand-Mère to worry about.

Sarah snapped her fingers. "How about a vacation? Go somewhere fun, like the beach. Have some drinks. Find a sexy guy to spend a week or two with, let him bang the memory of Ace right out of you."

I rolled my eyes, a slight smile playing on my lips. "Do you even know me at all?" I giggled, but it did spark another idea.

Maybe I could go to France for a while. I could do my work from anywhere, as long as I had an internet connection. I already knew enough French to get by, and we had lots of family still there. I was sure I could find a place to stay for a month. Or two. Maybe three? I didn't know. However long it took to heal my heart. I wouldn't have to be here in Nashville, hearing about the lawsuit against

Dalton Enterprises on the news or hearing about Ace's misadventures on a daily basis. I wouldn't have to risk running into him or his brothers if I wasn't in town.

The more I thought about it, the more France sounded like the perfect "next move" for me.

CHAPTER 12

Ace

*V*oicemail. Again.

I'd lost track of how many times I'd tried to call Callie, and each time it went directly to voicemail. Maybe she'd blocked my number? I sighed. Damn it, I had to talk to her. I had to try.

I was still holding my own personal court of misery in the library at the mansion, sitting around in pajamas and a robe all day, like I was Hugh Hefner minus the bunnies. I had started taking frequent trips outside onto the balcony to smoke, which Mother hated, but it helped my anxiety. My body was healing, slowly but surely, and I had started to feel restless. I needed to do something. I needed to talk to Callie—explain, apologize, grovel. I needed to try.

But she didn't want to hear from me. I cursed, tossing my phone onto the coffee table. How could I apologize if she wouldn't even talk to me?

I held my head in my hands, wondering if I stood in her yard, holding a boombox over my head while playing "In Your Eyes" like Lloyd Dobler in "Say Anything" if she'd let me in when I heard a faint knock at the door. I looked up to see Mother with Becky in tow. *Fuck*.

"Ace, sweetie, you have a visitor." I scowled at her while she motioned for Becky to come on into the room that had become my personal sanctuary. It felt wrong for her to be here after everything that had happened, so I sat frowning at both of them while Becky walked in. A low-cut dress hugged her curves. Her long blonde hair was pulled up into a ponytail, and the corners of her red lips tilted up in a tentative smile. She made herself comfortable in a wingback chair, looking around the room in wonder. I stared daggers at Mother as she left, oblivious to my displeasure, shutting the door behind herself.

"So, how are you feeling?" Becky asked quietly after finally tearing her gaze from the shelves of books surrounding us.

"Never been fucking better. Why are you here?" I was in no mood for chit chat, cutting right to the chase so I could hopefully get her the hell out of here as soon as possible.

She sighed. "Ace, I feel so bad about what happened to you. I knew this lawsuit was trouble for your family, but I never thought anyone would try to... kill you." She whispered the last two words, her eyes wide. She held the handle of a small tote bag, which she twisted back and forth while she spoke.

She thought the environmentalists jumped me at the gas station and beat the hell out of me? Wow. I wasn't sure what to do with that—if I should correct her, let her continue thinking it, or just laugh—when she interrupted my thoughts.

"I decided I couldn't live with myself if something happened to you when I could've prevented it. I mean, I work at the law firm. I should've found out as much as I could've for you before this happened. I'm so sorry, Ace." The words spilled out of her while her eyes glistened with tears. I winced. I couldn't let this go on in good conscience.

"Becky, it wasn't—"

"Don't ask me how, but I was able to gather some more information for you." She reached into the tote bag, pulling out a file folder. She thrust it at me, and instinctively I reached for it.

"What's this?"

"Everything is there. The whistleblower's name and the statements he gave. Basically, he tipped off the Environmental Council that Dalton Enterprises had begun testing a new method of off-gassing ethanol during the whiskey maturation process over the last few years, which caused the fungus to germinate much more quickly and more densely than it naturally would have." She recited it as if she'd memorized it from the statements inside the folder.

I thumbed through the file while she summarized the contents. This could actually help. This could possibly turn the lawsuit on its head if we could prove we weren't testing any new methods of off-gassing. Admittedly, I had no fucking clue what we were doing at the distillery, but I hoped it wasn't this. I closed the file folder and leveled my gaze at her.

"Thank you. I think this will really help, Becky. But I have to be honest with you," I said, running a hand through my bedraggled curls. "It wasn't the Environmental Council or anyone affiliated with them who attacked me. I appreciate your concern, though. You didn't have to do this." I pointed at the folder and gave her a small smile of gratitude.

She shrugged. "I hope whoever it was gets what's

coming to them. And you're welcome. I hope you can use the information. Also… I'm sorry if I caused any trouble by showing up at the hospital." She paused, biting her lip as if waiting for me to spill the details about Callie and who she was to me. *Fuck.*

I didn't want to talk about it, especially not with her. I shook my head and waved dismissively. "Don't worry about it."

Becky nodded and stood to leave, then turned around to face me only a few steps from the door. "Oh, if you hear of any job openings, let me know. I'm probably going to be fired over this." She giggled, then saw herself out.

I looked at the file folder, shaking my head with a wry smile. The time for licking my wounds was over. It was time for me to come out of my self-imposed hiding, suit up, and kick some ass. I needed to call a meeting with Dad and the golden boys pronto.

Ace

TWO HOURS LATER, NICK, JASPER, AND DAD WAITED FOR me in the library. They'd come straight from work, still wearing their suits and ties. I'd taken the opportunity to grab a shower and put on a suit, myself, in the meantime. I was about to hand Dad the information he'd been searching for all this time on a fucking silver platter. I finally felt like I had something to contribute to the company, so why not dress the part? I was still broke and in debt up to my eyeballs to my brothers, but I still had a closet full of designer clothes.

When I waltzed in, wearing a dark blue Armani suit,

silver rings catching the light, they all turned to stare at me. Dad with a scowl on his face, Nick smirking, and Jasper looking genuinely happy to see me. I still had some healing to do, but damn, it felt good to be back.

"What the hell is all this about, Horace?" Dad asked, his frown deepening the wrinkles around his mouth.

"You look great, Bro. Glad to see you getting back into the swing of things," Jasper said, smiling from ear to ear.

Nick stayed silent, still wearing that cocky grin on his face as if he were just waiting for me to fuck something up. I ignored him and focused on Dad.

"What's the one thing you've been searching for over the past few weeks, Dad?" I held up the file folder, just out of his reach. He frowned.

"Cut the bullshit. What's in the folder?" he barked at me.

"Did you get some information about the lawsuit?" Jasper asked incredulously.

Nick perked up at that, leaning forward in his chair. "Let me see it," he demanded, holding one hand out.

"I did. You're welcome. And hell no," I said, addressing that last part to Nick. I flipped the folder open, finding the part Becky had highlighted. "Read this." I handed it to Dad, Jasper and Nick immediately moving to crowd around him so they could read it too.

"Holy shit." Jasper's jaw dropped as he read before a slow smile spread over his face.

"I'll be damned." Nick finished reading, glancing up at me with a respectful nod. "Didn't think you'd pull it off."

Dad was still reading, flipping through all the papers in the folder, peering carefully over his glasses as he did. Jasper moved to the desk in the corner of the room, where there was a laptop. He sat down, fingers moving furiously over the keyboard, while Dad continued inspecting every document in the file.

I stood, sweaty hands clasped in front of me, feeling more anxious than I wanted to admit. I wanted this information to be the key, and I wanted to be the one who had brought it to them. But part of me was waiting for Dad to tell me it wasn't good enough. He couldn't use any of it. That would be par for the fucking course for me, so I steeled myself for it.

Finally, Dad straightened all the paperwork and placed it back in the folder neatly. He laid it on the coffee table in front of him, then turned to where Jasper sat, still working on the laptop. "Did you find it?"

"I was able to log in remotely, and I found the old records. We did test that method of off-gassing." Jasper gestured to the computer screen, which none of us could see from where we were.

"What? Fuck," I said, deflating. I sat down heavily on the couch, waiting for the rest of it. This information was useless. Once again, I was a failure, blah, blah, blah. I couldn't believe I let myself think this was going to be the key to the case. I ran a hand through my hair, sighing.

"We tested it in 1992 for two months. We stopped when we realized what was happening with the fungus. That method was also not giving us the results we were looking for in the final product, so we abandoned it. We haven't used that method since then, and we have plenty of documentation to prove it, including notarized inspection records." He beamed at me. "Ace, you did it."

The corners of my mouth began to lift in a tentative smile upon hearing Jasper's words. I glanced at Dad for confirmation and found him staring at me with a strange look on his face.

He nodded. "Thank you, Son. This is information we

can use, and we wouldn't have gotten it without you. I think we can get the cease and desist order overturned first thing tomorrow with this." A hint of a smile played on his lips as he stared at me with that look on his face again. Was that—pride? I'd never seen him direct it at me before, so I couldn't be sure.

Nick walked over to where I sat and clapped me on the shoulder. "Well done, Ace. We can get production going again, call back all the workers who were laid off. A lot of people have you to thank right now."

"Well done, indeed." Dad smiled at me, meeting my gaze for a brief moment of understanding that passed between us before turning his attention back to Jasper, leaving me reeling.

I did it. Well, technically, Becky did it. But they wouldn't have even known about her if it wasn't for me, so I'd gladly take the credit. It felt fucking outstanding to get to be the one who saved the day for once, and I was riding high and feeling good. My first instinct was to call Callie and share the news with her. Then it hit me. I sighed, my high not quite so high anymore but still feeling pretty damn good about myself.

I wanted to see Callie. I needed to see her, talk to her, explain all this stupid shit away. Admit that I'd fucked up and tell her I was sorry. But she wouldn't answer her phone.

I watched, deep in thought, as Dad, Nick, and Jasper huddled around the laptop, talking animatedly while pointing at the screen. They were happy, which made me happy. I'd solved this problem. Why couldn't I solve the problem between Callie and I, too?

An idea hit me. What did I have to lose at this point? Fuck it, she wouldn't answer her phone, but I knew where she lived.

Callie

ZIPPING UP THE LAST OF MY BAGS I'D PACKED FOR France, I looked around my bedroom at everything I was leaving behind to make sure I hadn't missed something important. Satisfied, I moved the bag to the closet with the others, where they'd be ready to go this time tomorrow when I'd be leaving for Paris.

I was scared, sad, and excited about leaving Nashville. The morning after Sarah sparked the idea, I had spoken to Grand-Mère and made some plans; it turned out one of our relatives owned an apartment building in Paris. After a quick phone call, he'd told us he had a vacancy, and it was mine for as long as I wanted it. We negotiated a great deal for the rent, and I'd booked my plane ticket the same day. I hated to leave my comfortable little home here in Nashville, and I hated to leave Grand-Mère, but I needed space. And Grand-Mère was more excited than I was about it, although sad about the circumstances. I thought she was eager to live in Paris again vicariously through me, which made me smile.

I made my way downstairs to the kitchen, where I poured myself a tumbler of whiskey, White Wolf, to be specific. How fitting, drinking my last night away in Nashville with the Dalton family brand. I took the bottle with me, settling down on the couch with the remote and a blanket. I pulled up the app on my phone for my favorite delivery service and placed an order for dinner, then started flipping through Netflix for something to watch. I had just finished off my second drink when I heard a knock at my door.

My stomach growled as I flung the door open, expecting to see a delivery person with my pasta order. Instead, there stood Ace Dalton, holding a bag from the restaurant while the delivery guy pulled out of my driveway.

Damn him, but he looked incredible. A black t-shirt clung to his muscular frame, offsetting his ink nicely. He wore a pair of black skinny jeans and sneakers, along with his signature silver rings and watch. That chiseled jawline, those piercing eyes, and those pouty lips. My heart did a little flip in my chest as I let my gaze drift up his body unabashedly. I hated myself for it, but I wanted to memorize everything about him in case I never saw him again. Maybe it was the effects of the alcohol, but I allowed myself to slowly drink him in.

When I finally met his sapphire gaze, saw that cocky half-smile on his face, I came to my senses and moved to slam the door. He was faster than I was, grabbing the door before I could pull it shut completely. I let go with a frown, allowing the door to swing open again. "What do you want?"

His expression turned serious as he held the bag out for me and said, "I just want to talk. Please?" I noticed there were still bruises and half-healed cuts on his face, dark circles under his eyes. The part of me that still cared wanted to ask how he was feeling, but I squashed that idea as quickly as it came. He held the bag out to me, his eyes pleading.

"What more is there to talk about, Ace? You made it clear that you didn't see a future with me." I grabbed the bag out of his hand, letting it fall to the floor next to me. I'd lost my appetite, anyway. "Please go."

I moved to close the door again, but he inserted his foot in the door jamb this time, his eyes never leaving mine.

"I lied, okay? That was a lie, and I want to explain everything to you. Please?"

Lied? I stared at him for an uncomfortable moment. He pushed his hands into his pockets, giving me a smoldering look as he waited for me to decide. I could say no, slam the door, and get back to my pasta and Netflix. I could leave tomorrow and possibly never lay eyes on Ace Dalton again. But that piece of me that still cared wanted to at least hear what he had to say, even if it was all bullshit. In the name of closure, I told myself. I took a deep breath and silently opened the door wider to allow him in.

As he slid past me, I caught the scent of sandalwood and tobacco, which made me go weak in the knees. God help me, I'd missed him so much. I gestured for him to sit while I grabbed another tumbler from the adjoining kitchen. I had a feeling we were both going to need a drink for this.

"You have five minutes. Talk." I poured us both a generous helping of whiskey. His fingers grazed mine as he took the glass from me, and I cursed myself for the way his touch made my skin tingle. I sat on the opposite end of the couch, turning my body to face him while taking a drink. The whiskey burned its way down my throat, leaving a warm sensation to settle in my stomach as I waited for his excuses.

He ran a hand through his curls, leaving them disheveled. "Callie, I should've told you everything from the start. I wanted to, but I was afraid of ruining what we have —had." He stopped, tossing the whiskey back. He examined the empty glass in his hand, smirking. "I fucked it up, anyway."

"Just say what you wanted to say, Ace." My heart squeezed as I watched him sitting there with his empty tumbler, looking like a lost puppy. He didn't seem to know what to say or where to start, and I couldn't help but feel a little sympathy for him. "Start at the beginning," I said softly. I grabbed the bottle of whiskey and moved closer, refilling his glass and mine.

And he did. He started with that night at the club, when he'd lost twenty thousand dollars to a guy named Andre in a poker game. He told me about meeting Becky and fucking her in the bathroom. How his father had cut off his credit cards the next day, demanding that Ace get his life together. How he'd started working for the family business, jumping through every hoop his father put in front of him. The embarrassment of the bachelor auction, the threats from Andre's men because of the unpaid debt, the lawsuit against Dalton Enterprises, his father's command for him to get information about the lawsuit from Becky, who it turned out, worked for the prosecuting attorneys. Everything leading up to the night he was attacked after leaving my house.

He stopped, giving me a solemn stare. I threw back the last of my whiskey, feeling quite buzzed. "Callie, I came here that night intending to tell you everything. I got scared. I was afraid I'd lose you if you knew exactly what a cluster fuck my life was." I held the bottle out to refill his glass, and he let me.

He met my gaze, his eyes burning into mine. "They would've come after you. I couldn't let that happen."

I finished pouring and set the bottle down heavily on the coffee table. I sighed.

"Ace—"

"They would've hurt you like they hurt me. Maybe worse. I couldn't take that chance, and that's why I lied and told you we couldn't be together. It had to be convincing. I had to do it. I lied, Callie. I lied." He looked at me with such pain in his eyes, pleading for me to understand. Pleading for forgiveness.

"You should've told me."

"I know."

"You should've trusted me."

"I know."

"We could've handled Andre. Together."

He sighed. "It wasn't that simple."

"Seems like it was as simple as paying him. Your brothers paid him, right? And it's over now. I could've helped you." I shook my head. It was too much. He was too much. I poured myself three more fingers of whiskey.

"I didn't know that then. I didn't know how far Andre would go. I'm sorry." He looked defeated, placing his still half-full glass on the coffee table.

"And Becky?" I asked, the words bitter in my throat.

"A means to an end, that's all. I swear, I never wanted to fucking see her again after Indigo. I had no choice."

I swirled the whiskey in my glass. "You know, they used to call this stuff 'southern poison.'" I glanced at him as I took a drink, feeling the whiskey's fire coursing through my veins. "It's just like you. I couldn't resist you—believe me, I tried. I wanted you, and you made me feel things I'd never felt before. But in the end, you were no good for me. Just like poison." I finished my glass, placing it next to his on the table. "Please. Just go."

"Callie, listen to me," he said with urgency, moving to kneel before me. He took my hand, and I let him, too weary to care by now. "I lied when I said we could never work. We work, baby. We're the *only* thing that works. You know it." He brought my hand to his mouth, placing soft kisses along my knuckles. I pulled away.

"No. Ace, you were right. We can't work. I can't trust you," I said. I stared into his blue eyes, full of pain, and I couldn't help myself. I reached out, caressing his stubbled cheek. He melted into my touch, closing his eyes. I leaned forward, placing my forehead against his. I let my fingers tangle into his curls, holding his head to mine. I closed my eyes, breathing him in.

This would be the last time, my goodbye to him. Me, closing this chapter. Closing the book on Ace.

I squeezed my eyes shut, letting my mouth find his. I kissed him softly as he cupped my face, letting his hand slide to my neck, pulling me closer. My hands roamed over his muscular arms, gripping his biceps. I pulled the t-shirt over his head, dropping it to the floor, then leaned back on the couch in invitation. He rose from where he still knelt in front of me, joining me on the couch.

His hands moved over my body with urgency, his mouth crashing against mine. In a blur of movement, my clothing joined his shirt on the floor. He made quick work of removing his jeans and boxers. I closed my eyes, letting my head fall back into the couch cushions as his lips blazed a trail over my skin—from my neck to my breasts, my stomach, lower still. I moaned as he found my core with his tongue, working it in slow circles, torturing my body and my soul as he did. My fingers threaded through his hair as I pressed him into me, my hips bucking to meet his every movement.

It was a beautiful torment; the perfect ending to what had almost been. A tear slid from the corner of my eye as I let myself have these last moments with Ace. I knew I'd be gone this time tomorrow, far away from him, his problems, and his lies. My traitorous heart wanted to forgive and forget, accept his apologies and continue like nothing ever happened. But for once, I had to look out for myself, guard my heart against its own reckless behavior. I'd barely pieced myself back together after Vic. I couldn't let my heart be torn apart again. I wouldn't let it happen again.

I was so close to falling over the edge when I felt Ace's hard length at my entrance. He pushed into me with a groan, falling forward to nuzzle my neck as he moved within me, stroking just the right spot to keep my momentum going. I dragged my nails down his back, wrapped my legs around his waist. I held him to me, wishing things were different. That he wasn't so complicated and that I'd never known heartbreak before so I could give myself to him, not knowing or caring how it could end.

With every touch, I said my goodbyes, withdrawing my heart from him a little more. Taking it back, what I'd mistakenly decided to give to him. It felt too heavy, like a massive burden, but I had to reclaim it before he destroyed me completely.

He pulled out as we found our release together, collapsing next to me on the couch, our hearts pounding, our skin slick with sweat. Another tear escaped, sliding down my temple into my hairline as I caressed his skin, tracing the linework on his arms, while sleep carried me away into dreams of Paris without him.

CHAPTER 13

Ace

I checked my phone again. Nothing. It had been three days since I'd left Callie's house, after confessing everything to her while we drank until our feelings bubbled up to the surface, culminating in the best damn apology sex I'd ever had. I'd carried her to her bed before I left, tucking the blankets around her when she didn't awaken. She hadn't exactly accepted my apology, despite the sex, and it hadn't felt right to stay there with her, not knowing where we stood.

Now, three days later, with no word from her, I was starting to get the message about where we stood. My heart was a stone in my chest, heavy and cold. I knew I'd fucked up big time, and I'd tried to apologize, to explain it all to her. It seemed I'd lost her, anyway.

I thought about Callie and what I should do next as I wrapped up work at the office. Since giving Dad the information about the whistleblower, his lawyers had succeeded in overturning the cease and desist order on production. Dalton Enterprises was back in business, and to show his gratitude, Dad had given me my own office and relieved Greg of his babysitting duties. I now had a real job here, and I was learning all about the business from Jasper and a few others in preparation for a new role. I wasn't sure what Dad had planned for me, but I had to admit that I didn't hate this new responsibility. In fact, I kind of enjoyed feeling like I was contributing to the family business and not being the resident fuck up anymore.

The lawsuit wasn't over, however. The Environmental Council wasn't giving up so easily now that they'd made national headlines by dragging Dalton's name through the mud and succeeding in halting our production, even if only for a short time. We knew they'd only try harder now, which meant we had to be ready.

For days, I'd been going through old records, searching for anything they may be able to dig up to use against us. I'd found a few insignificant violations and write-ups from inspectors over the years, and I'd turned them over to Nick for review. For now, that was my job, and I was satisfied with where my life was heading. Except for one missing part.

Fuck it. I slammed my laptop closed and grabbed my phone off the desk. I was going over there.

Callie

IT WAS RAINING IN PARIS. I'D BEEN HERE FOR THREE days and hadn't seen the sun shining yet, which was an accurate reflection of my soul. I'd unpacked my bags amid a cold chill surrounding my heart, trying to settle into the small apartment my cousin, Marc, had so generously allowed me to rent for next to nothing during my stay here. It was furnished and had a cozy vibe, but I just wasn't feeling it yet. I didn't know if I ever would, to be honest.

I pressed my forehead against the cold glass, watching the rivulets of rainwater flow down the other side of it. I watched people on the street below, rushing to escape the downpour with umbrellas or newspapers held over their heads. Cars splashing through puddles in the road as they sped past. This was all I'd done for three days. I hadn't even bothered to boot up my laptop to check emails from clients.

Fuck. I had to get it together. I'd made the decision to leave, now I had to live with it. I had to get on with life here in Paris and forget about Ace. Dwelling on the situation and how his lips felt on my skin only a few short nights ago wouldn't help me get over him.

I moved off the window seat, taking my laptop out of its bag to fire it up. I dug my phone out of my purse, where it had been stashed since I landed, and had texted Grand-Mère to let her know I'd arrived safely. Twelve missed calls and thirty-six text messages, most of which were from Ace. Damn it.

I needed coffee before I did anything else. Luckily, the kitchen in the apartment had a coffeemaker, and Marc had made sure the cupboards and refrigerator were stocked with a few staples upon my arrival, including coffee, cream, and sugar. I could've kissed him if he were here.

Just as I sat down in front of my laptop with a mug of fresh coffee, my cell phone vibrated noisily on the table. I picked it up, afraid I'd see Ace's name on the screen, but it was my best friend, Sarah, instead.

"Hello?"

"*Bonjour*!" she exclaimed with a giggle. I rolled my eyes but couldn't help smiling at her enthusiasm.

"Hey, babe, what's up?"

"You are in the most amazing city in the world. The question is, what's up with you?" she asked in a voice that was much too perky for my mood at the moment.

"It's raining." I sipped my coffee, opening up my email program on the laptop.

"Fuck that, you can still find some hot French boys in the rain."

"Sarah…" I started, shaking my head, although she couldn't see me. I had already told her that wasn't why I was here. I had no intention of seeking out "hot French boys" to take my mind off Ace.

"Babe. I just want you to have some fun while you're there, okay? Don't spend months in Paris moping over some shithead in Nashville."

"I know. You're right, but I've only been here for three days. Give me a minute, okay?" I laughed despite my heavy heart. I knew it would take a lot more than three days, but there was no use in trying to explain it to Sarah. She just didn't understand. Hell, sometimes I didn't even understand.

My heart begged me to abandon this crazy idea of living in Paris for the next few months. It pleaded with me to get on a plane and go back to Nashville, find Ace, and forgive him. It longed to feel his hands on my skin, his lips on mine. But my brain shut those thoughts down as quickly as they came. I had to stay away from him. If I went back now, it would only end badly for me. Ace would only end up wrecking me. It was inevitable.

"Fine," Sarah said, pouting. "But please try, okay? Oh, I've gotta go, babe. Call me soon? I want to hear good things next time we talk, okay?"

"I'll try. Love you."

"Love you too, babe."

I ended the call, tossing the phone onto the couch with a scowl. I didn't want to try. I didn't know what I wanted, except to get back in bed and pull the covers over my head. I picked up my mug of lukewarm coffee and made myself read some client emails, pushing all thoughts of Nashville and Ace Dalton aside for now.

Ace

I PULLED THE JEEP UP IN FRONT OF CALLIE'S HOUSE TO see her Mustang in the driveway, along with another sedan. An older woman was on the porch, carrying a garbage bag down the steps. I hopped out, approaching with a ball of anxiety in my stomach. Something was definitely off about this situation, and alarm bells were sounding in my head.

"Hello," the woman called, stopping at the bottom of the stairs when she saw me. She shielded her eyes from the fading sun with her hand, her gray-streaked brown hair pulled into a bun at the nape of her neck. She was tall and thin, and she flashed me a cordial smile when I stopped a few feet away from her.

"Uh, hi. Is Callie around? I'm Ace," I said, running a hand through my hair while looking up at the house. My gaze returned to the woman, whose eyes were strikingly similar to Callie's. This was her grandmother, I realized.

"Ace." The smile on her face faded as she pronounced my name with the hint of a French accent and disdain. She turned her attention back to the garbage bag, tying a knot at the top, then hoisting it up to toss it into the green trash bin next to the driveway. I shoved my hands in my pockets, waiting. I supposed her granddaughter had told her what happened between us, but I wasn't going to leave without seeing Callie first.

"She's not here." The older woman said finally, turning her attention back to me. She crossed her arms, cocking her head and staring at me.

"Her car is here." I nodded towards the Mustang in the driveway.

She smiled wryly at me. "I didn't say it wasn't. I only said *she* is not here."

I scoffed, irritation twitching at the corners of my lips. "Okay. Where is she then?" Clearly, the woman wasn't pleased to see me here.

She took a deep breath, letting her arms drop to her sides. "You broke her heart, you know. She had been so afraid to open herself up to love again, and I helped convince her to give you a chance." Her expression turned to disgust as she raked me up and down with her deep blue glare. "And look what happened."

I dropped my gaze to the ground, my hands still in my pockets. She wasn't wrong, and I felt like shit for it. "Look," I said softly, "I know I messed up. I messed up big time, okay? But I care for your granddaughter, ma'am. And I want to do whatever I can to make it up to her." I brought my gaze to meet hers, which had softened considerably, prompting me to continue.

"I was trying to protect her, and I went about it the wrong way." I dropped to sit on Callie's front porch steps, her grandmother still standing before me, listening as I continued to ramble. I scrubbed my face with one hand, my eyes stinging. "I couldn't let anything happen to her, and if that meant lying to her, telling her I didn't want her anymore, then that's what I had to do." I saw her shift as I spoke, one hand moving to rest on her hip. Once I started, I couldn't stop the words from falling out of my mouth. "I don't deserve her or her forgiveness. I know that. But I can't help wanting it. Wanting her."

She sat beside me on the step then, her hand covering mine with a gentle grasp. "Then never give up on her, *mon beau*," she said, her French accent growing heavy. "Give her a little time, then go to her. She's scared now. She needs time to miss you."

I turned watery eyes to Callie's grandmother, who looked so much like an older version of Callie herself, my heart squeezed. "Where is she?" I asked, voice hoarse with emotion.

She withdrew her hand from mine, shifting to face me. "Paris. She needs space, *bébé*. Let her have it for a while."

I nodded, absently picking at the trousers I still wore from work that day. "Okay. Okay," I said, still nodding, fighting back the goddamned tears that were threatening to fall.

Space. Time. I could give her that. For a while.

CHAPTER 14

Callie

I set aside the landscape painting I'd been working on all day for a client. It was almost finished anyway, but I had grown tired of looking at it. A cabin surrounded by snowy mountains and trees was not where my mind wanted to be today. Although it was turning out nicely, I noticed as I removed the canvas from my easel.

Six months. It had been six months since I'd laid eyes on Ace Dalton, and yet I couldn't let him go, not completely. I'd pulled myself from the depths of heartbreak not long after arriving here in Paris, deciding I'd take Sarah's advice and try to have some fun. Try to rid myself of the feelings I had for Ace. And I did have fun, for the most part. I'd made some friends in the apartment building and at the cafe across the street. Flirted with a few men who'd shown some interest in me. I'd even gone out on a couple of first dates, but nothing compared. There was nothing here that compared to what I'd felt with Ace, however fleeting it had been. And that was the harsh reality I had to face.

I ran away when things got difficult. Let fear keep me a prisoner. And now I lived with regret and my healing heart, safe from being broken again. But was living life cautiously, with a closely guarded heart, any way to live?

I pulled out the canvas I'd been working on lately in my spare time. I carefully set it on the easel, letting my eyes drink in the portrait of the man I'd loved. I had loved him, I had come to realize, in the months I'd been away. I painted Ace. The way I remembered him that night, I really saw him for the first time at Union Station. When I'd realized how dangerous he was for me, but I'd wanted him, anyway. I didn't want to forget anything about him, so I'd started painting him. His unruly curls, the strong angle of his jaw, his piercing eyes, and the smolder they held for me.

I missed him, and that was the hard truth. I regretted closing the door on him, on us. Yes, he'd made a mistake when he didn't tell me everything that was going on with him, didn't allow me a chance to help him. When he decided how to keep me safe from his enemies without consulting me. But I'd also made mistakes. And I'd made damn sure we never forgot them.

I chose a tube of Burnt Sienna, squeezing a bit onto my palette. I brushed it onto the canvas, my thoughts drifting back to the time I'd spent with Ace, the way I'd felt when I thought it was possible to love again.

I could text him. The intrusive thought echoed in my head. I pushed it away immediately. No, I couldn't. He'd probably found someone else by now, anyway. I had no right to reach out to him now. I continued painting, dabbing color onto the canvas in various places, losing myself in my memories of him. The words from his poem, which I'd written down that night, flooded my senses.

Her touch, a remedy, healing me
Her gaze, a bolster, strengthening me
Her kiss, a shield, protecting me
Unworthy, undeserving, unremarkable
Yet she sees something in me
Worthy, deserving, remarkable
Loveable

Tears blurred my vision as I laid down the palette and brush. I had to do something; I had to try. I'd been so stupid to throw away what Ace and I had because I was afraid. I allowed the tears to come, letting them wrack my body while I sobbed for everything we could've been.

After a few minutes, when I was all cried out, I picked up my phone. I scrolled through recent texts with Grand-Mère, Sarah, clients, and new friends here in Paris. I paused when I found the name I was looking for.

Ace Dalton.

I opened the long-dormant text message. He'd sent so many texts during my first few days in Paris, and I'd ignored them all. Eventually, he had stopped, my silence sending the clearest message of all. I began to type.

Hey you. How have you been?

I immediately deleted it.

I began again, with a simple "hi." I deleted that, too. I sighed, putting the phone down. I didn't know what to say to him. What was there to say now, anyway? I turned to stare at Ace on my canvas, his eyes haunting me. Maybe one day I could reach out to him, but this was not that day.

Ace

JASPER, NICK, AND I TOOK OUR PLACES AT THE LARGE table in the boardroom, next to our lawyers. Dad sat at the head of the table, steely gaze on the petite redheaded woman who strode in wearing a power suit, followed closely by two men and another woman, all of whom turned looks of disdain on us as they took their seats across the table from us.

"Ms. Emery," Dad's lawyer, Kenneth, acknowledged the redhead as she removed some paperwork from her brief-case. She nodded tersely in response. Instantly, I didn't like her.

"Shall we get started?" she asked, letting her gaze pass over everyone in the room, not actually caring whether we were ready to begin or not.

"Yes, please, enlighten us. Why are we here today?" Dad asked wryly, crossing his arms. His complexion seemed even paler than usual today. His jaws were sunken, and he seemed dwarfed by his Armani suit.

Emery turned a hateful glare on Dad, but before she could reply, the woman to her right spoke up.

"Mr. Dalton, I called this meeting in the hopes that we can put this lawsuit behind us. I'm assuming you'd like that as well?" she asked, her blonde hair pulled into a loose chignon, her green eyes cold. She looked at all of us in turn, stopping to stare at Nick for a moment longer than the rest of us, I noticed. I suppressed a smile, filing that bit of information away for later.

"I would love nothing better, Mrs..." Dad paused, waiting for her to supply her name.

"Ms. Martin. Amelia Martin. I'm the executive director of the Environmental Council's board."

"And what is your proposal, Ms. Martin?" Dad asked, leaning forward, eyes sharply focused on her.

She smiled tightly, cocking her head at him. She had classic good looks with fine features, and I was willing to bet she came from old money, a rebellious daughter trying to make her own mark on the world. *Join the club, sister.*

"It's simple, really. In fact, I can't believe none of us thought of it sooner." The two men on either side of her snickered while Ms. Emery kept her eyes trained on Dad. *This should be good.* I glanced between Dad and Ms. Martin, waiting for the fireworks to begin.

"I can't wait to hear it." Dad narrowed his gaze. I saw the little vein in his forehead begin to throb as the blood rushed to tint his face pink.

She smiled sweetly at Dad. "Dalton Enterprises only needs to relocate the whiskey manufacturing facility to a more rural area, leaving the metropolitan Nashville area to recover from years of fungus accumulation. We would be willing to financially join efforts with your company to assure Nashville is restored to its previous glory, free from the visual blight your product has inflicted on it for decades." She folded her hands on the table, meeting Dad's gaze with an intensity equal to his own. I pursed my lips to suppress a laugh. *Who did this bitch think she was?*

Dad silently stared at her while the rest of us waited with bated breath. I knew what was coming. Jasper and Nick probably did, too. Poor Ms. Martin had no idea what kind of wrath she had just unleashed, however.

"You want me to relocate? After I've spent years building this company, building relationships with this community, you want me to rip it all up by the roots and relocate? This is the 'simple' solution you came up with?" Dad's voice was low and smooth, his deep Southern accent punctuating every word with his distaste for the idea.

179

Ms. Martin—Amelia—cocked her head, smiling at him once again as if he were a young child who couldn't understand. "I assure you, Mr. Dalton—"

"You're wasting my time with this idiotic idea? I have half a mind to—" Dad bellowed before Nick jumped in, cutting him off, while Jasper restrained Dad from jumping from his seat.

"Ms. Martin, with all due respect, your idea is not a good one." Nick rose from his chair, motioning towards the door. "However, we will take it into advisement, and we'll get back to you with a counteroffer soon." I didn't miss the way Nick's eyes raked over Amelia Martin, admiring the way her skirt hugged her ass. She was a good-looking woman, no doubt, but what a bitch. Bitches always were Nick's type, though, I thought with a shrug.

"The hell we will!" Dad yelled, jerking his arm from Jasper's grasp.

"Dad," Nick said simply, holding one hand up in warning. "If you'll allow me to see you out, Ms. Martin." He again gestured towards the door, turning his gaze on the executive director and her minions.

Amelia frowned, glaring at us all, one by one. "Of course," she finally said, her voice icy as she conceded. Along with her lawyer and the others, she rose from the table to follow Nick out of the boardroom.

She paused in front of Dad, turning a fake smile on him. "We look forward to hearing from you, Mr. Dalton." Without waiting for a reply, she tossed her shoulders back and strode out of the room. Nick waited for her to slide past him, his eyes following her for a moment before turning to us to roll his eyes in amusement as he closed the door behind him.

Kenneth, Dad's lawyer, peered at Dad over his black-rimmed glasses. "That outburst is going to be all over the news, Augustus. She'll spin it as though you spurned a perfectly suitable solution. This could be bad. Very bad."

"I don't give a damn. I'm not uprooting everything I've worked for, the legacy I'm leaving to my children, to pacify some goddamned hipsters who've suddenly decided whiskey isn't green enough for them!" He slammed his fist on the table, jarring the entire room.

Nick walked back in just then, the amusement fading from his face as soon as he laid eyes on Dad. "Dad, I'll handle her," Nick said, moving to sit beside Dad. *Yeah, you'd like to*, I thought with an internal chuckle before turning my attention back to Dad and Kenneth.

"If you don't find a way to satisfy them and get them to drop this lawsuit, you're not going to have much of a legacy to leave them, anyway," Kenneth said with a sigh. "I'm sorry to be so blunt, Augustus, but you know it's true. And we don't have a lot of time left."

Collectively, we looked from Kenneth to Dad and back again in confusion.

"What's that supposed to mean?" Jasper asked, eyeing Dad.

Dad glared at Kenneth for a moment before sighing heavily. "I didn't want to tell you like this, but it looks like I don't have a choice now," he said, and if looks could kill, Kenneth would've been pushing up daisies already.

"Go on," Nick urged, his face pale as he glanced at Jasper and me, then back to Dad. My chest felt heavy suddenly, and a lead ball settled in the pit of my stomach.

"I have cancer. Stage four, nothing to be done about it now. The only thing I can do is ensure I'm leaving you with a profitable, stable company." Silence filled the room as we let the news sink in.

After a moment, I cleared my throat. "Dad…" I began, but he held up a hand in protest.

"No. We're not discussing it any further. We will concentrate on getting this lawsuit dropped and getting that bitch off our collective backs. Understood?" He turned his gaze on each of us in turn, ensuring we understood he didn't want to talk anymore about his diagnosis.

I nodded, followed by Nick. Jasper nodded and asked, "Mom knows?"

"She does," Dad replied curtly before turning to Kenneth. "I need you to keep working on this, redoubling your efforts. We need to counteract anything she says to the media."

Kenneth swallowed hard. "I'll do my best. You know I will."

Dad nodded again, his jaw clenching. His large, powerful, and intimidating frame suddenly seemed small, pale, and fragile in light of his news. I looked at Jasper and Nick, whose faces mirrored mine. Shock. Confusion. Sadness.

Now, more than ever, I wanted to earn my place at Dalton Enterprises. We had to put an end to this lawsuit, and soon—and I vowed to do everything I could to make that happen.

Ace

I THREW BACK A SHOT OF WHISKEY WHILE I STARED AT MY phone. I couldn't find the words I wanted, and the poem I was working on was swiftly turning to shit. I decided to put it away for now. Maybe it would come to me later. As I shoved the phone into my pocket and waved at the bartender for another drink, I spotted my brother heading towards me.

"At the bar after work... some things never change, do they?" Jasper asked with a grin as he took the seat next to me. The bartender made his rounds, leaving us both with tumblers of White Wolf. I tossed mine back while Jasper only took a sip, sitting his nearly full glass on the counter in front of us.

"What brings you to this den of iniquity, Jas?" I asked, knowing how he felt about my former lifestyle. I scowled at him, assuming he was judging me. The way I saw it, just because I was getting my shit together didn't mean I couldn't enjoy a drink at the bar now and then.

Jasper smirked, taking another drink. "We haven't talked in a while. You weren't at home, so I thought I'd find you here. I wanted to catch up, see how you're doing." That was my brother, the youngest golden boy, always worried about everyone else instead of himself.

I knew what he was getting at, though. What he really wanted to know was how I was doing since Callie left. And I wasn't sure I wanted to answer that question.

"I'm great. I'm loving my new job, and being sober ninety percent of the time isn't as bad as I thought it was gonna be. Loving life, man." I sat my empty glass on the counter heavily with a sigh. Lies, all lies.

He looked up from his glass with hooded eyes. "Have you heard from her?"

"Nope," I said simply, hoping to shut this line of interrogation down immediately. I should've known that would never work.

"Hmmm." Jasper took a generous gulp of his whiskey, nodding his head. "Don't you think it's time you got your ass over there?"

I sputtered. "Excuse me?"

"There's no use in playing dumb with me, Ace. I know you too well. You're not even close to being over her. So, go. It's been what, six months? She's had plenty of time to figure out what she wants." He tossed back the remaining whiskey in his tumbler. When the bartender glanced our way, Jasper motioned for another round.

I shook my head, a wry smile playing on my lips. "It's not that easy."

"What do you have to lose at this point? You don't have her, and you're not happy, so you might as well go to Paris and give it a shot." He shrugged, lifting the fresh glass of White Wolf to his lips as soon as the bartender turned his back on us.

I put my head in my hands with a sigh. What did I have to lose? My dignity, if she had, in fact, moved on and forgotten about me. She was in Paris, for fuck's sake, the goddamn city of love. Some asshole named Pierre had probably stolen her heart by now. He probably brought her croissants every morning while wearing a beret, and she hadn't spared another thought for me since stepping off the plane months ago. Who was I to barge into her new life, hoping she'd be willing to forgive me now? I didn't know if I could take the rejection if she had found someone new.

On the other hand, I'd never know unless I tried. Was I willing to let her go, never see her again? Never find out for sure whether any feelings remained? Was I willing to give up and let Pierre become her everything instead of me? Fuck no, I wasn't. The thought of her in another man's arms made me feel murderous. She belonged with me; I belonged with her. That was the simple truth we'd both been avoiding since the moment we'd met. It was time to stop fighting it, and if I had to strangle some French playboy with his own beret to win Callie back, I'd sure as hell do it.

I had to go to Paris. I had to find out how she felt now, even if she'd moved on. How could I ever move on without knowing for sure? How could I ever move on without her, period? I didn't think I had a choice anymore. I had to go. For the possibility of even the slightest chance that we could be together again, I had to go to Paris.

I looked up at Jasper, meeting his knowing gaze. His lips turned up into a smug smile as he drained the rest of his whiskey. "Want my travel agent's number?"

I rolled my eyes at him. "Yes. But there's something I have to do first. Then I'm Paris bound." I threw back the last shot the bartender had sat in front of me, letting the whiskey burn its way down my throat.

Maybe it would be a mistake, but I had to go. I had to try. I was ready to get on a plane right this fucking second, but I needed to take care of something first. Something I'd thought of doing the night I'd left her house all those months ago, and I'd never gotten around to it after things fell apart. After that, I'd board a plane to Paris and hope to God I wasn't too late.

CHAPTER 15

Callie

The warm sun felt nice on my skin as I walked home from the market, carrying bags full of fresh produce and bread. The Paris sky was clear and blue, not a cloud in sight. People wandered up and down the streets, in and out of shops. I shaded my eyes with one hand as I glanced at my surroundings, a slight breeze rustling my sundress. I loved having cafes and markets within walking distance of the apartment, and I was getting used to a routine I'd established here. Get up early, exercise, work on client projects, relax with a book and coffee at the cafe across the street, order in for dinner, and fall asleep watching whatever series I was currently binging on Netflix. It was cozy, but I had to admit, it was becoming boring.

As much as I loved Paris, I missed Nashville. I missed my little house with the large window upstairs. I missed my own bed and all my belongings I couldn't bring with me to France. I missed Grand-Mère and Sarah.

I missed Ace.

God, I was pathetic. Six months later and over four thousand miles separating us and I still couldn't get him out of my head or my heart. Everything reminded me of him. Everything made me wonder how he was doing. What he was doing. If he'd found someone new. My heart ached, begging me to reach out to him to find out if there was still a chance for us. As much as I wanted to, I couldn't bring myself to do it. It would destroy me to find out he'd moved on with someone else.

I'd learned a hard lesson about love from Ace, one I'd never forget. A broken heart is a risk you have to take if you want to find love. If you never put your heart on the line, you'll never find someone willing to risk it all for you, too. I was afraid after what happened with Vic, and I had let that fear make me pull back with Ace when things got difficult. It was safe, but in that safety, I'd lost my chance at love. Probably forever.

The day he came to me to apologize and explain, I had every right to be angry with him. But I should've worked through that anger. I should've listened to him, accepted his apology. There were a million things I should've done instead of booking the first flight to Paris to escape him. No matter what Ace had done, I only had myself to blame for running away instead of facing my feelings for him and trying to make things work. Ironically, I'd done it all to avoid a broken heart, yet here I was in Paris, and my heart was in a million pieces, anyway.

I tried to push thoughts of Ace aside as I approached my apartment building. I remembered the vegetables I'd purchased and thought of what I could cook for dinner tonight as I walked along the narrow sidewalk. I half-heartedly smiled at an elderly man as we passed each other. Then a little girl ran by, nearly colliding with me. I laughed as she shouted, *"Excusez-moi!"* but my amusement faded when I saw what she held in her hand as she continued running down the walkway.

A sunflower.

I stopped dead in my tracks, my eyes on the flower as the girl ran off into the distance with it. Suddenly, I was standing in my Nashville house again, staring at my unfinished sunflower painting with Ace by my side. He'd asked me why sunflowers were my favorite, and I'd told him about the Greek myth and how Clytie the water nymph had never stopped loving the sun god, Apollo, even though he'd cast her aside. She never took her eyes off Apollo as he moved the sun back and forth in the sky. In her sorrow, she eventually became a sunflower, destined to face the light of the sun forever, never forgetting her heartbreak.

I'll never get over him.

Hot tears spilled down my cheeks as I came to this realization. I clutched my bags tighter and sprinted towards my building. I needed to curl up in my bed, pull the covers over my face, and cry until there was no tomorrow.

I lunged at the stairs to the apartment building, flung open the door, and almost tripped when I saw another sunflower just inside. Was I hallucinating now? I ran to the staircase, taking them two at a time when I saw another sunflower... and another. They were like a trail leading me up the stairs. What the hell was happening?

I stopped at the landing, dropping my bags of fruit and vegetables to scrub at my eyes. My keys hit the floor, apples rolled down the stairs, and a loaf of fresh bread bounced out of the bag at my feet. But I didn't care. One hand flew to my mouth as I took in the sunflowers, my breath catching in my chest. I bent down to pick one up; I definitely wasn't imagining this. I began to walk slowly, following them up the remaining stairs to the floor my apartment was on. A feeling I hadn't dared let myself have in the last six months bloomed in my chest. Hope.

I bit my lower lip, a slow smile spreading on my face with every step, with every new sunflower I spotted. Fresh tears stung my eyes, but now they were happy tears. Hopeful tears.

He was here. He had to be. I picked up my pace, power walking at first, then jogging, then a full-on run when I turned the corner, and then... my heart stopped.

Ace Dalton stood by my door.

He looked as happy to see me as I was to see him. We stood, rooted where we were for a few moments, drinking each other in. He looked just like I remembered him, incredibly hot, with those smoldering blue eyes focused on me. The same disheveled curls, the same tattoos, the same stubbled jawline. A tight grey t-shirt clung to his muscled arms and chest while a pair of baggy jeans hung from his narrow waist. His silver rings glinted in the light as he turned to face me, a pained expression on his gorgeous face.

"I'm the fucking sunflower, Callie. Even when you're not around, you're all I see. I'm sorry for everything, and I'm sorry for showing up here like this, but I — "

I strode towards him as he spoke, finally cutting him off when I took his face in my hands and pressed my lips to his. I claimed his mouth, over and over again, with urgency and finality. This man I'd been so afraid to love had come for me after all this time. He was mine, and I was never letting him go again.

He kissed me back, scooping me into his arms, wrapping me up in his solid embrace. I let my hands roam over him, still in disbelief that he was actually here in Paris. Was I dreaming this? I tangled my fingers through his hair as we continued to kiss. I let them trace over his muscular arms, his chest, then back again to cup his face. This was real; he was here, and he still wanted me.

He finally broke the kiss, his hands on my face, thumbs caressing my cheeks. His eyes blazed as he met mine. "Callie. I love you. Please forgive me."

A sob mixed with a laugh escaped me as I looked at him. "I forgive you. I'm sorry, too. I'm sorry I ran away, and I'm sorry I was so damn scared of letting you in. I love you, too."

His mouth captured mine with a possessive kiss. His hands roamed over my thin sundress, teasing the skin beneath that had missed his touch. I moaned and let my hands slide down his back, his muscles rippling with every movement. I felt his hard length as I rubbed up against him, which ignited a long-dormant flame within my core.

"Are you going to open this fucking door or not?" he asked breathlessly, his voice thick with desire as he backed me towards the door to my apartment, still kissing and nuzzling my neck.

I laughed. "I dropped my keys somewhere back there," I said, gesturing vaguely towards the stairs. "The sunflowers distracted me." My keys were somewhere on the landing, alongside a couple of spilled bags of groceries. I couldn't have cared less at this very moment, though, as he continued to plant kisses on my lips and neck. I wouldn't have cared if he wanted to take me right here in the hallway.

"Fuck," he groaned. Releasing me, he stepped back and made quick work of kicking in my door, the knob shattering as it fell to the floor.

"Ace!" I laughed, covering my mouth with my hands. Marc, my cousin and landlord, was going to be so pissed.

Ace smirked, taking my hand to pull me inside my

apartment. "Tell your landlord I'll pay him double for it. Believe me, it's going to be worth it."

I laughed again, letting him lead me inside. He gripped my waist, pulling me to him, and kicked the broken door closed behind us.

Ace

"I'VE MISSED YOU SO MUCH, BABY," I SAID AGAINST HER lips, sliding my hands along Callie's skimpy sundress. We kissed, my tongue finding hers, while Callie navigated us towards her bedroom in the small Parisian apartment. Her hands roamed over my body, finally finding my cock, rubbing it through my jeans until I was hard as a fucking rock. This would not be some slow, romantic love-making session. There would be time for that later. This was going to be the "I've missed you so fucking much I need to be inside of you right now" sex that we'd both been waiting for.

We made it to her bedroom, knocking into various tables, the couch, and a few chairs along the way, our lips only parting long enough to draw air. When we reached the foot of the bed, she stopped, pulling back to look at me, biting her lip.

"You have no idea how much I've missed you, Ace. But I'm about to show you."

Her hands went to the button of my jeans, unfastening and unzipping, while she moved in closer to nuzzle my neck. She nibbled on my earlobe as she worked, breathing hard against my ear, making my cock even harder, if that was possible. My jeans fell to the floor, leaving me in boxers and my t-shirt. I reached behind my head, grabbing my shirt and dragging it up and off of my body. I tossed it aside while she helped me out of my boxers, freeing my cock.

I reached for her, but she dodged me, stepping back while pushing the thin straps of her sundress down her shoulders. She shrugged out of it, letting it drop, then stepping out of the discarded garment towards me. A sexy pair of white lace thongs and matching bra covered the parts of her I wanted to see most. Still, she looked gorgeous in them, the lace stretching delicately over every curve of her hips and breasts.

"Damn..." I drawled, my eyes raking over her body, taking it all in. A blush crept into her cheeks as I stared, gawked even, at this beautiful fucking creature standing before me.

Her long, mahogany-colored hair hung in loose curls, falling over her shoulders, providing the perfect offset to her creamy skin and the white lace she wore. Her dark blue eyes smoldered as she moved towards me, gazing longingly at my cock.

As I watched, she dropped to her knees in front of me, wrapping one delicate hand around the base of it, then giving it a few strokes before licking the crown. Her eyes met mine as she teased, swirling her tongue over me, making me shudder with anticipation.

"Callie," I said, panting as she wrapped those gorgeous lips around my cock. She took me in, letting her tongue slide firmly along the underside of my length as she sucked and teased. I gasped, tangling my hands into her long curls, holding her hair back out of the way as she worked. She moaned, sending a vibration through my cock, threatening to make me come right then and there.

I watched while she moved one hand to slip it under the lace of her panties while she continued sucking me. She worked her clit while licking my length, and if I thought I couldn't get any harder, I was wrong. The sight of her sinking her fingers into her core while she sucked my dick had me so fucking turned on. I had to get inside of her. Now.

"On the bed," I said, my voice husky with desire. I gently pulled her away from me by the hair I still clutched in one hand, then releasing her while she moved to the mattress. She lay back, propping herself up on her elbows, staring me down with a lazy smile.

"I need you, Ace. Right now." She sat up, her hands going behind her back to unclasp the bra, which she flung aside, releasing her full tits. With a growl, I moved to her, taking her mouth with mine, my hand cupping and kneading one breast, my fingers teasing her hardened nipple.

I nuzzled her neck, letting the feminine, floral fragrance of her perfume fill my lungs while I quickly removed the last scrap of lace that came between me and my woman. My woman. Fucking finally.

She stretched her gorgeous body out on the mattress, taking me with her, letting her nails rake down my back. A shiver went through me as I pushed into her opening. She moaned my name, her nails digging into the small of my back as I pushed in again, even deeper. Callie moved her hips to meet me, and soon we found our rhythm.

"God, you feel so fucking good," I said, grinding out the words as I lost myself in her soft folds. She wrapped her legs around my waist tightly as if to hold me there, but I had news for her. Nothing could make me stop now; nothing could ever make me let her go again. She was mine, and I was hers from now on. And I planned to prove it to her every fucking day of our lives.

Her breath came in short gasps, a sheen of sweat

covering her skin as we worked towards our release together. I claimed her mouth again, roughly, my tongue intertwining with hers.

"Ace…" she moaned, clinging to me desperately as I continued to pump into her, her hips still moving in time with mine. I panted against her neck, kissing the curve where it met her shoulder before whispering breathlessly.

"Come on, baby, come for me now," I said, feeling her inner walls gripping me as she let go, screaming my name. That sent me over the edge as well; I followed her over the cliff as we came together.

Thoroughly spent, I collapsed at her side, one arm thrown across her heaving chest. She drew closer, snuggling into me. I wrapped my arms around her, planting a kiss on the top of her head as she rested it on me.

I closed my eyes, imagining waking up every day like this from now on with Callie in my arms. I didn't feel terror or dread at the thought of being with the same woman for the rest of my life. Instead, it felt right. I felt whole. I felt complete.

"What's this?" she asked, tracing the tattoos on my arm with her fingers. I flipped my forearm over so she could get a better look at my new tattoo.

"I just got it a couple of days ago. Like it?" I grinned while the corners of her mouth turned up in a slow smile.

"You got a sunflower," she breathed, easing the tip of her index finger over it.

"I told you, I'm the fucking sunflower," I said with a laugh.

She raised up to look at me, shaking her head with a disbelieving grin on her face. She twisted to show me a patch of skin on her side that I'd been too distracted to notice while I'd been busy ripping her clothing off.

I leaned in to get a closer look at the lines of text I saw

on her skin. There it was, my poem, inked onto her gorgeous, creamy skin.

Yet he sees something in me —
Worthy, deserving, remarkable.
Loveable.

She leaned down to kiss me softly, tenderly. "Babe, I think we're both the fucking sunflower."

EPILOGUE

Ace

"Yes!" I cheered, jumping up from my spot on the couch next to Callie to pump my fists in the air. Jasper and Nick joined me as the Titans made the winning touchdown. I pointed at the television screen, shouting, "Fuck yeah!" Callie remained on the couch, laughing at my antics when I grabbed her hand to pull her up. I planted a kiss on her mouth as she continued to laugh, pushing me away.

"I'll never understand why y'all like this game so much," she said, rolling her eyes and swatting at me as I went in for another kiss. She looked so goddamn cute wearing a jersey and jeans, with her hair pulled up into a messy ponytail. I still couldn't believe she was actually mine.

"Stick around us long enough, and you will," Jasper said with a grin. He gave Callie a sisterly hug, ruffling her hair as she shrugged away with a giggle. Nick resumed smoking his cigar, watching us with amusement from a wingback chair in the corner.

I took in the scene around me with pride and awe. I hadn't spent time with my brothers like this since we were kids, and it was nice. We used to watch football together every damn weekend, but as we grew older and went our separate ways, that tradition had fallen by the wayside. I hoped today was the beginning of starting some new traditions with my family, which now included the love of my life.

It had been three months since I'd surprised Callie in Paris. Luckily for me, she forgave me and decided to move back to Nashville. We'd been inseparable ever since. Between my new job at Dalton Enterprises, which I was surprised to find myself enjoying, and coming home to this beautiful woman every night, I was pretty fucking happy with my life right now. The only thing that would make me happier would be to make it official with a ring and a date. And that was definitely on the horizon for us.

The four of us had commandeered the library at Mother and Dad's house to watch the game. Callie had made sure we had plenty of snacks and beer, so I went to grab a fresh Bud Light from the cooler when the library door burst open.

It was Dad, making his way into the room with his cane, followed by Mother. Both wore serious expressions on their faces. Dad looked weak, his skin pale and drawn, and he'd lost a lot of weight in the past few months. He reached a chair next to the couch and sat down heavily, with Mother by his side.

"What's going on?" Nick asked, putting down his cigar. He turned his dark eyes to me, and I shrugged. We both turned to Jasper, who seemed just as confused as we were.

Dad regained his breath while Mother wrung her

hands. "Turn on the news," he finally gasped, pointing at the television with his cane.

I grabbed the remote, changing the channel until I found the local news. It didn't take long to figure out what had our parents so bent out of shape.

There on the screen was Amelia Martin, the Executive Director of the Environmental Council's board. She looked as gorgeous as she had the day of our meeting, in a gray pinstripe suit, her blonde hair in a bun. A reporter held a microphone out for Amelia to respond to some question she'd already asked.

"Turn it up, Ace," Jasper said, eyes glued to the television.

I did as he asked. We sat silently, listening to her speak.

"Yes, we did offer a viable solution to the issue. Our team found acres of rural land Dalton Enterprises could have relocated their operations to, which would have moved the whiskey production facility far enough away from the metropolitan area to avoid the build-up of the Baudoinia fungus on our downtown buildings and monuments. Our foundation even generously offered to split the cost of the cleanup with Dalton Enterprises." Amelia's brow furrowed as she turned her teary emerald eyes towards the camera.

"Unfortunately, Augustus Dalton has refused to relocate, proving his company couldn't care less about the state of our downtown area and the toll this fungus is taking on our residents, our businesses, and our tourism. He may have managed to overthrow the cease and desist order on production, but we will not stop." Her jaw clenched, one perfectly waxed brow raised as her steely gaze seemed to stare right into my soul from the television screen.

"We will continue to fight. We won't give up. I hope the Daltons are ready because we're no longer asking nicely.

This is war." Amelia's hard gaze lingered as if she knew we were watching. In an instant, she replaced the hardass bitch face with a sweet smile for the reporter and said her good-byes. The reporter began wrapping up the piece, and I turned the volume back down.

Nick ran one hand through his hair, his expression murderous. "Fuck," he said. He shook his head, a smirk playing on his lips. "I should've known that bitch would pull something like this."

"She'll have every citizen of middle Tennessee signing a petition to have us relocate by tomorrow morning at this rate," Jasper said, standing to pace the room. Dad sat silently, watching, looking almost helpless. Mother patted his hand, looking as distressed as we all felt.

"Isn't there anything we can do?" Callie tentatively asked, looking from one to the other of us. I fucking loved how she said "we" and had to resist the urge to kiss her right then and there.

Dad sighed. "I've got Kenneth on the way over to discuss it." He slammed his fist against the arm of the chair, which took an effort he didn't have to spare. "It's horse-shit!" he bellowed, despite his obvious decline. Mother closed her eyes briefly, squeezing his hand.

"I'll take care of her, Dad. Don't worry," Nick said, his face hard. If I'd thought he had a thing for Amelia Martin at the meeting awhile back, I would say it was a thing of the past now. Not an ounce of amusement was evident in his gaze as he looked at all of us. In fact, he looked as if he would have no problem strangling Ms. Martin if he could get his hands on her at the moment. Whatever attraction there had been was over now that she'd declared war on our family.

Jasper stopped pacing. "I'll help. We'll figure it out, Dad."

I looked at Callie, taking her hand in mine. She gave me a soft smile, nodding. "We'll help too," I added, squeezing her hand. "This bitch picked the wrong distillery to fuck with."

Dad sat back in the chair, a satisfied look on his face. He smiled at Mother, then looked at all of us, one by one. "I'm proud of you, boys. All of you." His gaze settled on me with that last part. I couldn't help but grin back at him.

"Amelia Martin isn't going to know what hit her," Nick added with a cocky grin.

AFTERWORD

Stay tuned for the next books in the Tennessee Whiskey
Trilogy, coming in 2022!

Book 1 – Southern Poison
Book 2 – Southern Heat
Book 3 – Southern Honey

Did you love Southern Poison? Don't forget to leave a
review on Amazon and Goodreads! Reviews help indie
authors get their books noticed, we greatly appreciate them.
Thanks so much for reading and reviewing!

ALSO BY SHAUNA JARED

Nashville Immortals Series (Paranormal Romance)
Bitter End
Bad Blood
Burning Secrets

Anthologies her work is published in, all published by Tarina Anthologies:
Beautiful Apocalypse ("Southern Hospitality")
Beguiling Beasts ("Unrequited")
Love Sucks ("Closure" – A Nashville Immortals short story)
Mystical Maidens ("Born of Shadow and Light")

ABOUT THE AUTHOR

Shauna is a romance author who aspires to become a professional time traveler. Southern Poison (book one of the Tennessee Whiskey series), is her fourth novel and was published in August 2021. She also has a paranormal romance series, Nashville Immortals, with three install-ments published currently. Shauna is hard at work on her next book, book two in the Tennessee Whiskey series, as well as short stories for several anthologies. She writes about all things romance and lives vicariously through her characters.

Shauna lives near Nashville, TN with her husband, son, their dog, and a beta fish. She loves books, coffee, wine, and bacon, in no particular order.

www.shaunajaredauthor.com
    instagram.com/shaunajaredauthor/
    facebook.com/shaunajaredauthor
    twitter.com/shaunajared

Join the newsletter: https://lp.constantcontactpages.com/su/OnRPAXi/ShaunaJared

Made in the USA
Middletown, DE
17 September 2021